AVALANCHE!

I can't believe I did that, Lyssa thought as she felt Blue's haunches make contact with the tree trunk. Blue spooked, leaping sideways, then whirling to meet his enemy in a primal reaction to the sudden sound. As he did so, his shoulders brushed against a sapling, snapping it in such a way that the sound it produced was like a rifle shot.

"Easy there, Blue," Lyssa called frantically, struggling to control the frightened horse, who began plunging wildly.

Lyssa applied a pulley rein and fought to bend Blue around her leg, crooning in his ear the whole time, "It's okay. It's okay."

A few seconds later Blue stopped plunging, but Lyssa continued to turn him in circles till she felt sure his panic had passed. For a few moments she breathed in deep gulps of the frigid air, trying to slow down her wildly tattooing heart.

Whoa. That was close, Lyssa thought.

It was then that she saw a huge slab of snow break away, falling as if in slow motion. For an instant Lyssa stared, mesmerized, before it suddenly registered in her brain what she was seeing.

"*Avalanche!*" Lyssa cried out, turning Blue's head.

Collect all the books in the Thoroughbred series

Collect all the books in the Ashleigh series

*coming soon

THOROUGHBRED

HOOFPRINTS IN THE SNOW

CREATED BY

JOANNA CAMPBELL

WRITTEN BY

KARLE DICKERSON

HarperEntertainment

An Imprint of HarperCollinsPublishers

HarperEntertainment

An Imprint of HarperCollins*Publishers*
10 East 53rd Street, New York, NY 10022-5299

This is a work of fiction. The characters, incidents, and dialogues are
products of the author's imagination and are not to be construed
as real. Any resemblance to actual events or persons, living
or dead, is entirely coincidental.

Produced by 17th Street Productions,
an Alloy Online, Inc., company

HarperCollins books are available at special quantity discounts for bulk
purchases for sales promotions, premiums, or fund-raising.
For information please call or write:
Special Markets Department, HarperCollins Publishers Inc.,
10 East 53rd Street, New York, NY 10022-5299.
Telephone: (212) 207-7528. Fax: (212) 207-7222.

ISBN 0-06-009048-0

HarperCollins®, ®, and HarperEntertainment™
are trademarks of HarperCollins Publishers Inc.

Cover art © 2002 by 17th Street Productions,
an Alloy Online, Inc., company

First printing: December 2002

Printed in the United States of America

Visit HarperEntertainment on the World Wide Web at
www.harpercollins.com

1

"Two bags of Ajax HorsePower and a rubber curry-comb. That'll be sixty-four dollars and eighty-five cents," said Tess MacIntosh, the owner of Beartooth Feed and Seed, as she rang up Lyssa's purchase.

Seventeen-year-old Lyssa Hynde, who was standing at the worn wooden counter at the feed store she'd been coming to ever since she was a little girl, bit her lip as she counted out the bills to her father's old friend.

Whoo-ee! Blue, you definitely are worth it, but your supplements sure are getting to be expensive, she thought, catching a glimpse of herself in the horseshoe-shaped mirror over the register. Peering closer, Lyssa saw that her blue eyes were dark with worry. So she smiled broadly, not wanting to let on that she was freaking about finances these days.

"Here you go," she said to Tess with false brightness, handing over her money and picking up her new currycomb.

Tess smiled back. "I know you've heard this a hundred times, honey, but everyone here in Montana is so proud of how you and Soldier Blue took first place back east," she said, referring to Lyssa's recent win at the three-day event at Deer Springs in Kentucky. "We just know you'll be riding in the Olympics soon."

Lyssa felt her heart swelling at the thought of the incredible spirit her horse had shown during the tough competition in November. Cheering slightly at the compliment, Lyssa thanked Tess and turned to wait for her bags of supplements to be brought up from the storage area. She was shivering in her goose-down vest, so she stamped her moccasin-clad feet against the floorboards to warm up and inhaled the familiar smell of leather, hay, and grain. Her eyes wandered around the interior of the store that had once been the town's only livery stable. Now it served as a popular supply outlet as well as a gathering place for area ranchers.

Lyssa's gaze rested on a nearby bulletin board where local ranchers posted notices of equipment for sale or missing livestock. Usually the notices were about rustled cattle, but sometimes they were notices for horses. Lyssa frowned as she noted that there were several stolen-horse bulletins. It seemed that lately she'd heard about more missing and stolen horses.

MISSING: REGISTERED QUARTER HORSE MARE

STOLEN FROM SKY COUNTRY STABLES:
ONE THOROUGHBRED GELDING
REWARD

LOST OR STOLEN: TWO SHOW HORSES,
LAST SEEN NEAR COYOTE ROAD
REWARD FOR INFORMATION LEADING TO RECOVERY

Shaking her head, Lyssa peered at the accompanying photos, and her heart ached. She'd keep her eyes open, she decided. Maybe she'd get lucky and spot one of the missing horses wandering across the ranch land. Horses broke out of their pastures plenty of times and turned up on neighboring properties. Stolen horses, however, were rarely seen again.

If anything ever happened to Blue, I'd just die, Lyssa thought fiercely. *But first I'd find whoever took him in the first place and whomp that person.*

She took comfort in the knowledge that horse

thieves would find it pretty hard to rustle anything from Black Thunder Ranch, where she lived. Even though the ranch sprawled over hundreds of acres, there was always some member of her family or trusted ranch hand on the property. And the barn dogs barked like crazy anytime anyone set foot on the ranch.

Gazing out the window at the leaden January sky, Lyssa decided that for once the weather reports were right: They definitely were in for a snowfall.

I hope I make it back to the ranch before the snow begins, Lyssa thought, glancing at her watch. She was driving Tin Annie, her uncle Cal's old truck. The rusty old workhorse was pretty temperamental, so Lyssa wanted to be home before any kind of bad weather hit.

Mentally Lyssa ticked off the things she needed to do at the ranch. First she needed to bring in the geldings she'd turned out in the main corral before heading into town. Next she needed to give Blue a serious grooming session. Then she had to give a jumping lesson to fourteen-year-old Timorie Randall, who lived nearby. Afterward she needed to help Mitch Lightfoot, the lead ranch hand, finish soaping and oiling the tack that the dude ranch guests had used over the holidays. Then it would be stored until spring. Sighing, Lyssa hoped there were enough hours of daylight left.

There's always something to be done on a working ranch

that doubles as a dude ranch, Lyssa mused. But she wouldn't have it any other way. Her family had owned the land for several generations, and it was an inseparable part of her. Her pride in the land extended beyond the ranch boundaries and took in Montana as a whole, including the Beartooth Mountains, which rose majestically to the west. She'd ridden through the mountains for years and knew the trails better than almost anyone around her. She couldn't imagine living anywhere but Montana, though lately she'd found herself thinking it would be nice to travel internationally—specifically with the U.S. Olympic eventing team.

Lyssa's thoughts were interrupted by a sharp bark. She glanced over at a huge plastic crate that stood next to the snow shovel display. Someone had placed a sign that read Free to Good Home—Shots, Tests, and AKC Papers on top of the crate, which contained a partly grown Great Dane puppy. Frowning as she crouched down to peer through the wire grate at the fawn creature with a sweet black mask, Lyssa wondered, as she always did, how someone could bring home a pet, then decide to get rid of it—and not really care that much where it ended up.

Really, anyone could come in here and adopt this puppy, Lyssa thought, scowling. *And there's no guarantee they'd take care of it properly.*

Briefly she considered taking the pup home.

No, I'd better not, she thought, deciding against it. Money was just too tight at the ranch. Her dad was trying to stretch the budget to hire another hand to help with the work. Anyway, she and her parents already had so many animals to take care of. And judging from the size of this pup's paws, it was going to be huge.

"Ooh, look," said a little girl, sticking her fingers through the grate and tickling the fawn-colored dog's floppy ears. "Dad, can we have him?"

"How many times do I have to tell you we don't have any place to keep a dog, let alone one that size?" sighed her exasperated father, leading the little girl away.

"What do we have here?" said a woman's voice crisply from behind Lyssa.

Lyssa turned as a thin, sharp-looking woman wearing a filthy yellow jacket came up to the box. She looked to be in her forties, and her dyed blond hair was pulled back severely. The woman's eyes darted furtively from the sign to the puppy whining inside the crate. Lyssa frowned as the woman opened the crate door, pulled out the puppy roughly, and looked him over, prodding his ribs and poking his mouth to see his teeth.

"Probably would cost a fortune to feed, but could be

worth a lot of money to someone," she muttered under her breath. "I'll take him!"

The woman's words made the hair on the back of Lyssa's neck prickle.

"Excuse me," Lyssa said smoothly, taking the puppy from the woman. "I've already spoken to my friend Tess about adopting this big guy."

She looked over at her old friend, who was watching the exchange from the register, and shot her a look that she hoped conveyed a thousand words.

"It's true," Tess lied without missing a beat as her husband appeared with Lyssa's bags hoisted over his shoulder.

"But *I* want him," the woman snapped coldly, glaring at Lyssa.

Lyssa didn't back down. "*I* already claimed him," she replied, meeting the woman's cold stare.

"Gerald, would you help Lyssa load up her dog?" Tess said sweetly to Mr. MacIntosh.

Lyssa smiled inwardly as Mr. MacIntosh set down the sacks and pried the puppy from her hands. "Sure, I'll help you load *your* dog, Lyssa—and a bag of Nutro for him."

I can't believe I'm bringing home a puppy, Lyssa thought a few minutes later, dumping the big bags of Ajax into the back of the truck and climbing into the driver's seat. She spread out her old Navajo saddle blanket next to her, and Mr. MacIntosh set the puppy on it. As Mr. MacIntosh walked off, the puppy plopped down, gazing at Lyssa adoringly.

"You're way huge," Lyssa said, rubbing his ears. "My mom and dad will be less than psyched that I've brought another homeless animal back to the ranch."

Glancing at the puppy's big, trusting brown eyes, Lyssa knew she'd done the right thing. Something about that woman had given Lyssa the creeps. She never could have let her walk out of the store with any living creature.

"Now I guess I'll have to name you," Lyssa said sighing, stroking the dog as she pulled out of the parking lot. "Your papers said you're called Ruggins Velocity, but puh-*leez*. I just can't see myself shouting, 'Here, Ruggins Velocity!' We've got to think of something else."

Rolling down the window, Lyssa breathed in the familiar, tangy note of impending snow in the air while she coaxed Tin Annie out toward the highway.

"It's going to start snowing any minute now," she murmured.

While Lyssa drove toward Black Thunder Ranch, she watched as a number of fat snowflakes began to drift lazily from the sky. The sharp outlines of the Beartooth Mountains gradually softened in the haze of the gentle snowfall. In a short while, Lyssa knew, the brown, barren landscape around her would be still and white. There would be a hush over the countryside. Smiling, Lyssa thought of her beloved horse, Soldier Blue. How he loved to gallop through fresh powder!

Well, why not? Lyssa decided, grinning widely. *I'll get this pooch settled in the kitchen and whip through everything as fast as I can. Then Blue and I are going out for a ride. Fitness gallops, here we come!*

Drumming her fingers against the steering wheel in time to the music on the radio, Lyssa pictured how Blue would snort and nose the fresh powder. She imagined herself swinging easily onto his back and dashing across the ranch. They could start at the trailhead, where the land was level and smooth. It was the perfect place to gallop for miles without worrying about hidden rocks or holes. All around, it would be eerily quiet, and she'd have time to think, really think, in the way she could only when it was just she and the horse she loved more than almost anything in the world.

Just then the engine in the old truck made a horrible sound.

"Oh, no, you don't, Annie," Lyssa crooned uneasily, eyeing the gauges on the dashboard. "We've got to make it up the hill."

But at the base of the grade leading to the ranch, the

truck stalled. Lyssa got out and kicked the old contraption, then climbed back in. Luckily, when she turned the key in the ignition, the engine started again. Although the truck sputtered when Lyssa drove under the sign at the entrance of the ranch, it didn't die until she pulled up to the ranch house.

I wonder how much it will cost to fix the old girl this time, Lyssa thought glumly, opening the door and gathering up the Great Dane puppy in her arms. She'd begun worrying about money several years ago, when her father had gotten injured and her family had nearly lost the ranch. Things had eased up when they'd turned the ranch into a dude ranch, but then Lyssa had started showing Blue, and that meant traveling farther from home for more serious competition. Now that Lyssa was trying to secure a spot on the U.S. Olympic eventing team, expenses for competing were mounting more quickly than ever, and she knew that she'd have to do something about earning more money soon.

"I guess there's time enough to worry about finances later," Lyssa said aloud to the wriggling puppy. She wrapped him in her saddle blanket, but the pup was so big, his back end still remained exposed to the snow.

"Yoo-hoo, I'm home," Lyssa called out as she stepped through the door of the kitchen.

Marcy Hynde, who had Lyssa's same thick black hair and blue eyes, raised her eyebrows when she saw what Lyssa was holding.

"Don't ask," Lyssa said, setting the pup down on the linoleum.

Mrs. Hynde's eyes softened as she watched the big creature amble over to her, tripping over his huge paws in his eagerness to sniff her. "Oh, Lyssa, you just can't say no to animals, can you?" she said.

Lyssa grinned. She could see her mom was already falling in love.

"I tried to walk away. Really, I did," Lyssa explained, handing her mom the Kennel Club papers. "Someone was giving him away at the feed store, papers and all. And this nasty woman tried to snag him. I just couldn't let this sweetie go to her."

Mrs. Hynde set the papers on the counter and ran her hands over the puppy's smooth coat. "I don't blame you," she said. "But he's going to be as big as a horse, you know. Well, welcome to the Black Thunder, pup. What's his name?"

Lyssa shrugged. "Still working on it. The papers say Ruggins Velocity, but I'm going to have to come up with something better."

While the pup sniffed around the kitchen floor, Mrs. Hynde turned back to the big enamel pot she was stirring on the stove. "Three-alarm chili for lunch," she said. "Good and hot for this cold, snowy weather."

Lyssa nodded and walked over to peek into the pot. "I think you made enough for an army. You keep forgetting we don't have any dudes to cook for," Lyssa said, sniffing the spicy aroma of the chili. "Not till spring, anyway."

Mrs. Hynde laughed her light, silvery laugh. "It does take some getting used to, not having a pack of ravenous city slickers to refuel every few hours."

"Well, keep it hot, Mom. I'll grab some in a while," Lyssa said, heading for the door and pulling her Thinsulate parka from its peg. "I've got to bring some of the horses in before the snow really starts coming down. Keep an eye on puppy breath, will you?"

"I will. And by the way, your dad and Cal are out looking for a couple of horses that broke through the fence in the upper pasture," Mrs. Hynde said. "When they get back, tell them to come in for lunch."

"Okay," Lyssa replied as she pulled on her lined work gloves.

"Oh, the phone lines are back up again," said Mrs. Hynde. "Gabriela called."

Lyssa paused, her hand on the doorknob. *Ugh,* she groaned inwardly. *The community dance is tonight. Gabriela will want to know if I'm going.*

12

Just before the phone lines had gone down in a violent windstorm, Gabriela had called and begged Lyssa to come to the dance.

"I know you're busy, but you've *got* to come," Gabriela had pleaded.

"I don't know," Lyssa had said, not sure if she could stand another boring dance at the hot, stuffy grange hall. It sounded anything but appealing.

"Everyone's going to be there," Gabriela had insisted.

"Yeah, but don't you get tired of dancing with the ranchers' sons you've known your whole life?" Lyssa had complained to Gabriela.

"I, for one, am not going to be dancing with any locals," Gabriela had said mysteriously.

Lyssa had no idea what she meant by that remark, but she'd managed to be vague about whether she'd be able to make it. She'd been hoping that something would come up so she could beg off. Now the dance was upon her, and she didn't have an excuse.

"She's going to bug me to go to the dance tonight," Lyssa sighed.

Mrs. Hynde looked up from the stove. "She didn't mention anything about a dance, but she said she's got to talk to you. She's riding Fury over, so it may take a while."

Lyssa was puzzled. Why was her friend riding fat little Fury? Even though the Lattimers' ranch was a half mile down the road, if Gabriela was riding Fury, it could take forever. Fury belonged to Gabriela's little brother, Mattie, and he was part quarter horse. In contrast to Fury's romantic, energetic name, he was a lazy, squat fuzzball who hated to go any faster than a walk. "If you ask me, the other part has got to be turtle," Gabriela often said. Her horse was a beautiful eventing prospect named Mystic, and Lyssa couldn't understand why Gabriela wasn't riding her instead.

As she walked down to the wooden barn, Lyssa felt irritable. Lately Gabriela had been acting pretty weird. Lyssa couldn't quite put her finger on it. It had started when Gabriela began blowing off her eventing lessons without explanation. As her instructor, Lyssa had tried to understand. After all, Mystic had recently been having problems with on-again, off-again lameness. But one afternoon when Gabriela had missed a lesson and Lyssa had ridden over to the Lattimers' ranch to see what was wrong, she had spotted Gabriela on Mystic trotting alongside some guy who was riding Fury. Mystic sure hadn't been lame that day.

But maybe she's gone lame again today, Lyssa thought. *Poor Gabriela. Poor Mystic.* The moment Lyssa had set eyes on the elegant black Thoroughbred at an auction she'd stopped at on the way back from a three-day event in California, she had fallen in love. Mystic, with her athletic abilities and impeccable pedigree, had been way too expensive for Lyssa's pocketbook. However, she had promised to keep an eye out for a horse for Gabriela. Knowing the odds were that Mystic was too expensive for Gabriela, she decided to take a chance anyway and call her from a pay phone. She had been thrilled when Gabriela's parents had given Lyssa the green light to buy the mare for her. Though it wasn't the same as owning her, at least Lyssa would be able to work with the mare and see her whenever she wanted.

That is, until Gabriela had started blowing off her lessons and Mystic had started going lame. Lyssa hadn't paid much attention when Gabriela first switched farriers, but now that she looked back on it, the trouble had started soon after that.

"You ought to call the vet and see what the problem is," Lyssa had said to her friend the first time Mystic went lame.

Gabriela had shaken her head. "My parents spent so much money buying her, I don't dare hit them up for the money for a vet. I'll just try resting her for a few days and see if she gets better," she had said. "I'm too busy for lessons this week, anyway."

Lyssa hadn't approved, but when Mystic recovered, she forgot about the lameness and continued working with her. Then the lameness had recurred just before a local three-day event, and Mystic had to be scratched. Finally Lyssa had persuaded her friend to call a vet, and recommended Dr. Dealy, the equine specialist in Billings.

"You know I can't," Gabriela had said. "My dad always uses Dr. Maynard."

Lyssa had never cared much for Dr. Maynard. In her opinion, he always seemed to be rushed and in a hurry to get to his next call. Lyssa had driven over to the Lattimers' the morning of the visit, and the vet spent a few minutes with the mare, giving a cursory examination. "Pull her shoes and rest her for a week," he'd said briefly before taking off.

"I can't pull Mystic's shoes," Gabriela had said after he left. "I just had them put on. I'll rest her, but that's it."

Privately Lyssa thought Gabriela wasn't paying enough attention to Mystic's problem, but she tried not to butt in any more than she already had. She kept hoping that soon they'd get to the root of the lameness and Mystic could continue her training.

As Lyssa neared the main corral, she searched for the horses she'd turned out that morning, but she didn't see them. Putting her fingers between her teeth, Lyssa whistled shrilly. Immediately the ground shook

16

as four horses appeared from behind a clump of trees and tore toward her. They stopped just short of the rough-hewn log fence, nipping at each other's thick winter coats and squealing to get to Lyssa first.

"Take it easy, you guys," Lyssa called laughingly to the hairy, multicolored horses, who were jealously vying for attention. Lyssa led the horses into the roomy barn, putting them into thickly bedded stalls. Every time she walked past Blue's stall, he whinnied shrilly, pawing the floor.

"I'll be right with you, you spoiled thing," she called to her horse. "I know you hate being shut into a stall, but I'm not having you wandering all over the place in this freezing weather."

When Lyssa had put away the last of the horses, she made her way to Blue's stall. Opening his door, she stood for a moment, regarding the big, flea-bitten gray gelding standing squarely in his deep, thick bedding. At seventeen-plus hands, Blue nearly dwarfed her. His head was enormous, and his ears were large and floppy. He had a huge barrel and hooves the size of soup plates. Much as Lyssa loved Blue, she knew no one could ever call him handsome. But as an eventer, he was unstoppable. Bold, brave, and responsive, he could jump any fence, no matter how big or solid it was.

Blue was handy at dressage as well. Once he stepped into the arena, his massive frame took on a surprising elegance. He moved with grace and power, combining fire with restraint, rhythm, and balance. He was, as Lyssa proudly told her family and friends, a once-in-a-lifetime horse.

"What do you say, big guy? Are you ready for a gallop in the snow?" Lyssa asked, hugging her horse. She rubbed his shoulder, noting how his thick hair stood on end to better trap the warm air against his body.

Blue whuffed softly and nibbled at her shoulder with his soft, velvety muzzle, and Lyssa laughed as he tickled her. She pulled out her new rubber currycomb. "First we have to tackle this woolly fur coat of yours," she said, moving the comb in a circular motion at his withers.

"Hey, Lyss," called Mitch, the ranch hand, walking into the barn. He dumped a load of tack onto the tractor that served as a tack rack. "I'm ready to start our tack-cleaning marathon whenever you are."

Lyssa looked out the opened stall door at the ranch hand, who was shaking the snow off himself like a dog. Mitch was two years older than Lyssa and powerfully built, with wavy brown hair. When Lyssa was in middle school and Mitch had started working at the ranch, she'd had a huge crush on him, but over the years they had forged a brother-sister relationship and were fiercely protective of each other. They tended to tease each other mercilessly, to the point where sometimes they didn't speak to each other for days. But mostly they worked side by side, comfortable around each other and inclined to forget that they weren't siblings.

"Leave me a stack to do later," Lyssa said. "Work can wait. I'm just aching to take old Blue here out this minute and lay some track in this white stuff. I've got to hurry if I'm going to have time to ride before I have to give a jumping lesson."

Mitch's eyes traveled toward the window. "I don't know, Lyss," he said. "It's going to come down for real out there."

Lyssa tossed back her thick black braid and snorted. "Like I'd let a little sprinkling of snowflakes stop me?"

Mitch rolled his eyes and picked up a bar of saddle soap. "Why do I ever try to tell you anything?" he joked. "As for me, I'm staying put."

Just as Lyssa walked out of Blue's stall to grab a hoof pick, she heard the jingling sound of a bit outside the barn. Blue's ears pricked, and he gave a low whinny.

"It's Gabriela and Fury," Lyssa said loudly to Mitch. "If they're not afraid of a little snow, why should I be?"

"Hey, Lyssa, you there?" called Gabriela.

"In here with Blue," Lyssa called back. "And Mitch is burrowed in here, too. The big baby doesn't want to go out in the bad, bad snow!"

Lyssa scooped a handful of shavings from a nearby bag and tossed it playfully at Mitch as Gabriela led Fury into the barn.

"Hi, Mitch. Hi, Lyssa. Whoa—is it frigid out there!" Gabriela exclaimed, her cheeks flushed and her brown eyes sparkling from the cold. She had a light dusting of snow on her dark brown hair. Tying Fury with a slip-knot to an eyebolt, she walked over to Blue's stall.

Lyssa smiled at her friend, but she could see now that Gabriela was nervous and bursting to talk.

"What's up?" she asked. "Why are you riding Fury?"

Gabriela started to say something when the barn phone rang loudly, sending two of the more nervous barn dogs under a pile of feed sacks for cover.

"I got it!" called Mitch, reaching for the phone, which was perched on an oil drum by the tractor. He answered, listened for a moment, then held out the phone and said, "It's for you, Gabriela."

Gabriela raised an eyebrow. "Who in the world?" she asked, then rolled her eyes. "Bet it's my mom. You know what a major worrier she is," she added in a stage whisper.

20

As she picked up the receiver, she grimaced and looked meaningfully at Lyssa. "Hi, Mom . . . Yeah, I made it here safely." She twisted a lock of her dark hair. "Really, it's not that bad out there," she protested.

Mitch mouthed, "Oh, yes, it is" just before he walked out of the barn to get more tack.

"Oh, come on, Mom . . . Fine, I'm leaving now!" Gabriela hung up the phone, scowling.

"Aren't parents the biggest pain?" she asked Lyssa, placing her hands on her hips. "My mom wants me to ride home right now. Can you believe it? She says the weather's getting uglier, and she doesn't want me out in it."

"But you just got here," Lyssa protested.

"And I needed to talk with you—about Mystic," Gabriela said. "But I guess it can wait."

Lyssa frowned. Something told her it was better if they didn't wait.

"Tell you what. I'll ride home with you," she replied. "You can tell me on the way."

And I'll get to ride back alone—just me and Blue! Lyssa thought with satisfaction, rushing over to grab her sheepskin bareback pad.

2

"JUST GIVE ME A SEC TO GET READY," LYSSA SAID.

Quickly she finished grooming Blue. After picking out his hooves, she sprayed a can of nonstick cooking spray into his soles, saturating his frog so that the snow wouldn't ball up in his feet. She didn't want snow and ice to get packed around Blue's tender soles. Not only was the accumulated ice difficult to chip out with a hoof pick, but it could also throw off a horse's balance. What's more, the resulting decreased flexibility in the fetlock could cause a painful wrench as well. The nonstick spray helped loosen the snow so that it could be removed more easily.

"May I borrow a little of that?" Gabriela asked, reaching for the can so that she could spray Fury's hooves.

When Gabriela was finished with the fuzzy little horse, Lyssa shoved the can in her pocket along with her folding hoof pick so that she could stop periodically and check the horses' feet along the way. She knew how important it was be extra careful with hooves during the winter.

Soon Lyssa and Gabriela were mounted on their horses and cutting across the expanse of Black Thunder Ranch toward the Lattimer land.

Tilting her head upward, Lyssa caught a few snowflakes on her tongue. "Nectar of the gods," she cried, closing her eyes and feeling the cold air nip her cheeks.

Gabriela grinned as she adjusted her stirrup and nudged Fury firmly. "You've been reading Greek mythology again, haven't you?"

Lyssa had been home-schooled for the last couple of years because of her eventing schedule. It had been impossible to stay in school and travel to compete in the regional competitions. "You got it," she said, leaning down to pat Blue's neck. As was her habit, her eyes swept back and forth while she rode, taking in the gentle snowscape that was forming around them.

"You know, Lyssa, I sure miss having you at school," Gabriela remarked, leaning over to lift the baling-wire loop that held the gate at the other end of the main corral.

Lyssa slapped her gloved hands together for warmth after replacing the loop once she and Blue had ridden through the gate. "Once in a while I kind of miss school, too," she admitted. "I miss you and Amy and Kyla and the rest of the lunch table gang. But I'm glad I can learn at my own pace—and I'm glad I'm not cooped up inside a stuffy classroom anymore. I don't think I could stand it."

"Lucky you. You don't have to listen to Mrs. Snore Bore," Gabriela added with a laugh, referring to her history teacher. "But maybe you'll see her at the dance tonight. I hear the old battle-ax is chaperoning."

Lyssa frowned. "So everyone is still planning to go to the dance?" she asked.

Gabriela nodded. "I just hope my parents don't freak out about the snow at the last minute and make me stay home. I'm meeting my boyfriend there."

"Boyfriend?" Lyssa asked with a curious grin. "You didn't tell me you had a boyfriend."

Gabriela smiled. "Well, it wasn't official until a couple of days ago. His name's Brendan. He just moved here a few months ago. Plays basketball. Absolutely to die for."

That must have been Brendan I saw riding with Gabriela that day, Lyssa thought, looking over at her friend's sparkling eyes. She adjusted her sheepskin pad and sighed. She hadn't found a guy worth getting bright-eyed about since she'd met Parker Townsend in Kentucky. Good-looking as he was, he just wasn't quite right for her. Never mind that he lived hundreds of miles away. He was too arrogant and rich. And anyway, he was off-limits—he was taken by her friend Christina Reese, who lived at a Thoroughbred breeding and training facility near Lexington.

Briefly Lyssa wondered how Christina was getting along these days. She had recently come to stay at Lyssa's ranch to sort out her racehorse, Wonder's Star, after he'd gotten deathly sick. Lyssa had spent some time helping Chris and Star reestablish their bond, and Lyssa hoped that at last they were on their way to racing glory. After all, Christina had big dreams for Star, just as Lyssa had big dreams for Blue.

I'll have to e-mail Christina and get an update, Lyssa thought as she rode on, steering Blue through the fresh powder.

Blue's long, ground-eating stride quickly outpaced Fury's slow, plodding pace, and by the time the girls were near the highway, Lyssa had to stop and wait for her friend to catch up. She watched as Fury poked his way through the snow, his bright brown coat standing out against the whiteness around him. Gabriela, Lyssa noted, looked almost comical on him, her long blue-jeaned legs hanging well below his barrel in spite of his generous girth.

Finally Gabriela fell in behind Lyssa, sighing with impatience at Fury's reluctance to move out.

"So you didn't answer before. Why aren't you riding Mystic?" Lyssa asked her friend as she twisted around so she could hear.

Gabriela's eyes darkened. "Well, you're not going to like this, but I had to retire her," she said with a sigh.

"What?" gasped Lyssa. Mystic was only five years old. She was way too young to be retired.

Gabriela rushed on. "Come on, Lyssa. Don't act so surprised. You know her lameness just wasn't getting better. I can't keep resting her forever. She'll probably be lame on and off for the rest of her life."

Lyssa felt as if someone had kicked her swiftly in the gut. Looking away from her friend for a few seconds, she absorbed the news. Then she turned back. "You don't know that for sure," she said mechanically. "You only had that vet out one time. Maybe there's something to her lameness that we just haven't considered. I've said it before—you really ought to X-ray her."

Gabriela shook her head miserably. "As it was, my parents flipped when they got Dr. Maynard's bill. Especially since he didn't have a clear diagnosis. And X rays aren't cheap, you know."

Lyssa sighed. "I know. Vet bills can really mount up." She rode for a few moments in silence, then added, "It's just that now I feel terrible because I was the one who suggested you buy her in the first place. I called you from California and sang her praises to you, so you could hardly refuse. Now look—it ended up being one huge mistake."

Gabriela shook her head. "Don't blame yourself for one single second. I bought Mystic of my own free will," she said. "The purchase report was absolutely clean. No one could have guessed that a few months later she'd go lame. It couldn't be helped."

Lyssa slapped her gloved hand angrily against her thigh. Sometimes horses were such heartbreak! All her dreams and plans for Mystic would now have to be put away. It was too much.

"But there's good news," Gabriela went on. "I found an amazing home for her."

"What?" Lyssa exclaimed. It never occurred to her that Mystic wouldn't be retired on the Lattimer land, turned out to pasture with their other horses.

Gabriela held up her hand. "I know what you're thinking," she said. "But it's impossible. My parents are having enough trouble making ends meet, and my dad said there's no way we can have a nonworking horse eating her head off on the ranch."

Lyssa had been a rancher's daughter long enough to know that philosophy. Raising cattle and horses on the range was a hard life. There simply wasn't enough money to spare to spend on horses that weren't useful.

"So where will Mystic go?" she asked.

Gabriela's face lit up. "That's the good part. Amy told me about this woman—her name's Mrs. Peters—who has a big spread near her. You know, the Fowlers' old place. I guess she started renting it after her husband died, and she rescues animals. Anyway, I brought Mystic over there a couple of days ago. Mrs. Peters is a real character. She has more animals than you can imagine—horses, some cattle, dogs, and a whole bunch of cats. She loves animals and keeps them forever. The barn's full of them, and she's set up all kinds of kennels as well."

"Wow," Lyssa said. "Tell me more."

Gabriela urged a resistant Fury forward again, who responded by switching his tail and flattening his ears. "Not much more to say. But you'd like her. She's just like you, and she can't go anywhere without bringing home a stray."

"Speaking of which, I adopted a dog today," Lyssa cut in. "He's the cutest Great Dane puppy."

Gabriela's throaty laugh rippled around them. "Never enough animals for you, are there?" she teased.

Lyssa grinned. "No. And the feed bill at the feed and seed will confirm that."

"Well, anyway," Gabriela went on, "Mrs. Peters was really sweet about Mystic and said she'd live out her days as her big pet. She'd feed her carrots daily and love her up and everything. . . ." Gabriela's voice trailed off, and she gulped.

Lyssa sighed. "I wish it had turned out differently," she murmured sympathetically.

"Mrs. Peters says we can go visit her anytime we want," Gabriela said brightly.

"Let's do that—and soon," Lyssa said.

As happy as she was that Mystic at least had found a good home, Lyssa was filled with frustration as they continued on their way toward the Lattimer ranch. She couldn't help thinking that Gabriela hadn't explored every possible explanation for Mystic's lameness. If only Gabriela had used her vet, Dr. Dealy. He had been treating the horses at Black Thunder Ranch for years, and he'd diagnosed all kinds of baffling cases. But Lyssa knew that Mr. Lattimer and Dr. Dealy hadn't spoken in years because of some old grudge left over from their high school days.

It was all so ridiculous, Lyssa thought. And now it probably meant that Mystic was retired before her time.

Still, Lyssa knew, it wasn't her decision to make. She'd have to respect her friend's ultimate right to do what she thought best.

Oh, Blue, Lyssa thought, leaning down to wrap her arms around her horse's neck, *I'd just curl up and die if anything happened to you. But even if it did, you'd always have a forever home with me. I don't care how much Mrs. Peters loves animals. It can't compare to the love you get here.*

Bright lights shone from the weathered Lattimer ranch house as the two girls approached the ridge overlooking the house. To Lyssa, the lights pooled on the sparkling snow looked like one of those nostalgic paintings the mall stores sold that had names like "Welcome Home." Still, Lyssa thought, looking away from the house and toward the mountains, the Beartooths rising in their coat of white behind the house were definitely more inviting.

Nearing the house, Lyssa could see Mrs. Lattimer standing outside the front door, motioning Gabriela to hurry up.

"So much fuss about a little snow. I'm surprised my mom didn't send the posse after us," Gabriela commented dryly. "She's a world-class worrywart."

"Parents can go a little overboard sometimes," Lyssa agreed, though she had to admit her mom and dad weren't quite the worriers that Gabriela's were.

When the girls stopped their horses in front of Gabriela's mom, Mrs. Lattimer handed them each a cup of hot cocoa. "You must be absolutely freezing," she said.

Lyssa took the cup and giggled, shaking her head. "It's not so bad," she exclaimed after sipping. "I'm wrapped from head to toe in Thinsulate. And Blue has a coat like a grizzly bear."

Mrs. Lattimer screwed the top onto the Thermos. "Well, you two put your horses away and come on in to thaw out."

Lyssa surveyed the darkening sky. "Oh, I should probably get going," she said.

"You're not riding back in this storm," Mrs. Lattimer said in a commanding tone.

"This little ol' sprinkling isn't much of a storm, Mrs. Lattimer," Lyssa said, laughing merrily. "Now last winter, *that* was a storm."

Gabriela's mom pressed her lips together. "Okay," she said. "But wait here. I'm sending you back with the cell phone—just in case."

With that, she ran into the house.

Gabriela let out her breath loudly. "Aagh," she muttered. "She makes me crazy."

"Aw, don't worry about it," Lyssa exclaimed. "It makes her feel better if I carry it—even if everyone knows the reception is terrible around here."

After Mrs. Lattimer handed her the cell phone, Lyssa shoved it into her roomy pocket, where it clanked against the can of nonstick spray.

"I'll be fine," she said, then waved at Gabriela. "See ya at the dance tonight!" With that, Lyssa turned Blue toward home.

Making her way through the ankle-deep snow, Lyssa grinned. She looked up at the beckoning hills. It had been so maddening to plod along at Fury's pace. Now she and Blue were alone, free to fly like the wind!

"Come on, big guy," she called loudly to her horse as they started out across the rise behind the Lattimer land.

Blue took off like a shot, nearly unseating Lyssa. Inhaling the tang of snow, Lyssa felt her senses heighten as Blue gathered speed. The wind stung her cheeks, and her eyes teared. Wiping the tears away quickly so they wouldn't freeze, Lyssa let out a whoop that was quickly muffled by the falling snow. She was filled with the delicious exhilaration of the four-beat of Blue's powerful gallop.

"Oh, Blue, isn't this perfect?" she cried, leaning close over Blue's rhythmically pumping shoulder.

Minutes later she pulled up, her adrenaline rush

beginning to recede as she fell under the spell of the calm, frozen world around her.

Somewhere a wolf cried, and Lyssa shivered. Eyeing the white swirl around her, she saw that the snow was beginning to fall more quickly. Maybe it was time to turn for home, she thought.

Blue stamped his hoof and worked his bit, eager to set off once again. *Go home now?* he seemed to say.

"No way!" yelled Lyssa. "Yee-*ha!*"

With that, she touched Blue's sides, and the two of them tore along the fresh powder, sending up a white spray on both sides as they set off toward the Montana horizon.

3

LYSSA LET BLUE HAVE HIS HEAD, AND THE BIG HORSE slowed only when they neared the highway. Out of the corner of her eye, Lyssa could see several big rigs chugging their way up the grade. A couple of snowplows passed them, their lamps glowing an eerie yellow. The drivers waved at Lyssa, and she waved back.

As they got to the rise, Lyssa could see Black Thunder Ranch, enveloped in a blanket of snow. From her vantage point, the floodlight at the corner of the barn made the surrounding snow glisten like diamonds.

"What do you think, Blue? Doesn't it look like a magical fairyland?" exclaimed Lyssa, pulling up her horse, enthralled by the sight of her home dressed in winter finery. "The barn could be a castle, and our house the gatekeeper's cottage. The indoor arena is where the knights of old would have held jousting tournaments. And the creek winding around—don't you think it looks like a moat?"

She stopped for a moment to take in the enchanting sight, then turned to gaze at the cross-country course, now slowly being shrouded in white. She could barely make out the fallen logs or the hay wagon. The water jump had been frozen since late October. She'd have to wait months before she'd be able to climb aboard Blue and tear over the big obstacles.

I don't think I can stand to wait till spring, Lyssa thought, closing her eyes and imagining she was galloping over the course, the adrenaline flowing and the wind whistling in her face. There was nothing like the feeling of Blue gathering himself and making a mighty effort to negotiate a particularly big fence. While she daydreamed, Blue pranced around impatiently. Opening her eyes, Lyssa turned him in small circles, bending him around her leg while she fought to stay in her dream world.

Finally she forced her thoughts to return to the present, and she and Blue set off at a walk, turning toward a trail that led across the ranch.

"We'll go on over to the arena so we can do some dressage work," Lyssa explained to her gelding. "Won't that be fun?"

Sucking in the cold, stinging air, Lyssa looked around her happily. The trees were bare now, and their dark branches stood out in sharp contrast to the leaden sky. Looking down at the ground, she could see a few animal tracks, but for the most part the fresh powder was unmarred.

Suddenly she wished she hadn't agreed to go to the dance. Even seeing her friends didn't make up for an evening spent suffocating in a hot, stuffy hall. She would much rather spend the time hanging around home and getting to know the new puppy a little better.

Twisting around on the sheepskin pad, Lyssa looked behind her at the hoofprints Blue was leaving in the snow. They were large and rounded, set down evenly, and they told the story of his ground-eating, swinging walk. Lyssa had learned the art of tracking from her Native American grandfather. Glancing now at Blue's prints, she felt the gentle ache she always felt whenever she happened to think of her grandfather. How she missed him.

He had always encouraged her to dream, from the time she was a tiny girl. "Lyssa," he'd say soberly, "always ride the high country, where the view is forever and you're free to dream as big as the sky."

Smiling, Lyssa decided that her grandfather would probably be pleased that she had dared to dream of the Olympics. After cueing Blue, she skimmed the trail at an extended trot.

It was nice to have some quiet time for herself, Lyssa thought. Lately she'd hardly had time to breathe, what with Blue's rigorous training and competition schedule. And when she wasn't working with Blue or traveling with him to eventing competitions, she was working at the ranch, giving lessons to a few local students, helping her parents with the livestock, and entertaining the guests. Now that the dudes had gone home for the winter, there was a little more free time, but not much. And spring, though it seemed a long way off, would in reality come more quickly than she imagined.

"We're going to be so busy then," Lyssa said aloud to her gelding. "You and I have a lot of work to do to get ready for Rolex. We've just got to impress the Olympic selection committee."

Blue snorted as he walked steadily, sending up gray puffs of breath.

"I know," Lyssa muttered, running her hands through Blue's mane, now damp with snow. "You're just as worried as I am. How will we ever get it all done? Even if we don't sleep, we have more to do than we can ever hope to accomplish in twenty-four hours!"

She rode along, lost in thought. When she absently stuck her hand in her jeans pocket, she felt some crumpled paper and pulled it out. It was the receipt from the feed store. Sighing as she looked at the total again, Lyssa began mentally calculating the expenses she and Blue had racked up lately. Aside from feed, there were entry fees and extra shoeing bills as well. Two weeks ago the farrier had put special borium shoes on Blue to help maintain his traction in the snow. Those had cost half again as much as Blue's regular shoes.

And there was another problem as well. Uncle Cal's trailer had hauled its last horse over the holidays. It had become too rickety and dangerous, and Lyssa knew she'd have to rent a trailer for her upcoming competitions.

I could teach a few more lessons per week and try to save up for a new trailer, Lyssa thought. But then she shook her head. It was impossible. She simply couldn't squeeze anything else into her busy schedule.

She had promised herself not to worry about money for a while, but she couldn't help it. It all seemed to be nearing a crisis point.

There had to be some way to earn the money she needed to compete, she decided firmly.

Glancing up at the Beartooth Mountains rising in front of her, Lyssa studied them. She remembered what her grandfather had said about how they had been standing since the earth was young. They were invincible and unyielding, he'd added. Though they had been chipped away for centuries by the cutting effects of the relentless elements, they stood steadfastly, never letting any forces get the best of them.

"If they can stand up to adversity, so can I!" Lyssa said aloud.

Then she was struck with an idea so incredible, she stopped breathing for a moment. She would search for sponsors! Hadn't Tess at the feed store said people were still talking about her exciting win at Deer Springs? Over the last two months she'd heard a number of compliments like that one. Surely some business owners would think it a good idea to sponsor such a winning combination of horse and rider. Lyssa could advertise their products at the horse shows she traveled to. In return, they could provide her with the items she needed to stay on the Olympic campaign trail—things such as new tack or feed.

"What do you think, Blue?" Lyssa asked, her excitement mounting. "I could start with the feed store. The MacIntoshes might be thrilled to give me a hand in exchange for advertising. Or maybe Ajax Feeds might. After all, I buy enough of their products."

Of course, Lyssa didn't dare dream she could cover the expenses of a new trailer, but still, she felt her spirits rise. Getting sponsors might not solve all her money concerns, but it sure was a start.

Grinning broadly, Lyssa rode on. It was amazing, she decided. She could always come up with the best ideas when she was by herself, riding her beloved horse against the harsh backdrop of a snowy Montana day. Some people thought Montana's winters were dark, cold, and lonely. For her, they were a magical time, bringing forth excitement, new challenges, and at times even fresh bursts of inspiration. Why *not* dream of a new trailer? Maybe, just maybe, she'd figure out a way.

Visualize it and you can achieve it! she told herself. After all, that's what she always told her riding students.

Lyssa had just closed her eyes and pictured a shiny new trailer hauling Blue to Kentucky when suddenly Blue's body seemed to bunch up and he stopped short, his nostrils flaring. Opening her eyes, Lyssa looked around quickly, trying to determine the cause of Blue's abrupt stop.

"What is it, big guy?" she asked softly.

Then, just ahead on the trail, she saw them: fresh hoofprints in the snow.

"Huh. That's odd," Lyssa murmured, looking intently at them. "No one else is out here. At least I didn't see anyone."

Tilting up her chin, she wrinkled her nose. Suddenly she remembered her mom talking about her dad and Cal searching for some of their horses that had gotten out.

"No way," she said, dismissing the thought that these hoofprints might be theirs. "They wouldn't be out in this direction. The upper pasture is on the other side of the hill."

Squeezing her heels lightly into Blue's sides, Lyssa studied the prints as they walked along. They weren't deep impressions, which led Lyssa to believe they were those of a light horse. Delicate and rounded, they certainly weren't the prints of any of the sturdy cow ponies they kept on the ranch.

"And anyway, there's only one set," Lyssa added. "All right, Blue. We've got a mystery on our hands. Let's follow them and see where they go."

Blue seemed eager enough to go on. He pawed the ground impatiently, reminding Lyssa that she ought to check his feet again.

Lyssa jumped off, pulling out the folding hoof pick from her pocket and chipping at the snow that had balled up in Blue's feet. She didn't want to risk muscle strain that could be caused by snow packing around his frog and causing him to step unnaturally, as if he were walking on high heels.

Then she mounted again, and she and Blue followed the prints down through a gully and up to the other side.

Curiosity driving her on, Lyssa considered the possibilities. She flashed back to the missing-horse bulletins tacked up at the feed store. Maybe she was hot on the trail of one of those horses.

"How cool would that be, Blue, if we could find a missing horse!" Lyssa exclaimed.

Then her imagination kicked into high gear. Perhaps the tracks belonged to a stolen horse! Lyssa could picture herself bringing some criminal to justice—and raking in a little reward money as well. Maybe there'd be enough reward money to buy a new trailer.

"Dream on," Lyssa groaned, shaking her head at her ridiculous thoughts.

More likely she was dealing with a local rancher's horse who'd broken through a weak spot in the fence. Of course, that delicate shape certainly didn't belong to a cow pony, she reminded herself.

Lyssa stopped anytime she saw broken branches or twigs, examining them closely. Soon they were crossing a large field just before Six Creeks High School, where she had attended ninth grade before she began being home-schooled. Had one of the students ridden to school? Lyssa wondered.

Wait a sec—it's Saturday, she realized. *There's no school today.*

As the high school loomed into view, Lyssa could see that the parking lot was deserted. That meant there weren't any school events taking place that might explain the hoofprints. Her eyes traveled over the buildings that were frosted with snow as she made her way toward the front lawn.

A sign on the fence read Trespassers Forbidden on School Property at All Times. Lyssa glanced at it, then clucked to Blue as she rode forward.

I'm not trespassing, she told herself. *I'm tracking. There's a difference.*

Training her eyes on the tracks, she continued across the lunch area. Looking up, she scanned the classrooms around her, but she didn't see any signs of life.

"Yoo-hoo," Lyssa called out, listening as her voice bounced back and forth against the walls.

Making her way across the baseball field, Lyssa

continued to follow the hoofprints. Just past the field the prints turned and stopped abruptly at a covered sidewalk leading to the gymnasium.

Approaching the gate leading to the locker room, Lyssa swung down from Blue's back. Throwing his reins over his head, she led her horse along the sidewalk toward the equipment shed next to the gym.

Just as she rounded the corner, she heard a deep male voice yell out, "Whoever you are, get out of here!"

Lyssa lurched to a halt as a lanky young guy jumped out at her from behind the shed, waving his arms. He was wearing a green fleece vest that picked up the color of his flashing green eyes, and his jeans had a gaping hole in the knee.

"Get out of here—now!" he repeated in a voice that sounded like a growl.

Lyssa narrowed her eyes as she took in the guy's black cowboy hat and lean, muscular build.

Her first thought was, *He's amazingly good-looking*. Her next thought completely overrode the first one: *He's up to something—and it's definitely something no good!*

4

"ARE YOU BRAIN-DEAD?" THE GUY YELLED WHEN LYSSA didn't budge. "I'm talking to *you!*"

Lyssa crossed her arms in front of her chest. "My brain is alive and kicking, thank you very much," she replied hotly. "You're the one who's brain-dead if you think you can scare me by bellowing like a bull moose!"

The guy stepped toward her. "You're on school property!" he thundered. "And I'm not supposed to let anyone on the grounds."

"You don't look like a security guard," Lyssa shot back. *You look like a horse thief,* she thought. He was definitely hiding something.

"Whatever," the guy growled. "I'll radio headquarters if you and your horse don't leave now."

"Look," Lyssa said in a softer voice, her eyes sweeping around, looking for prints, "I'm not here to break in or anything. I'm tracking a horse. The hoofprints led here, and I just *have* to see if I can find him."

The guy drew himself up to his full height. "Horses? There aren't any horses around here," he said flatly. "Now scramoose!"

Lyssa held up her hand. "Maybe I will, maybe I won't," she muttered, grabbing Blue's mane and swinging up on his back.

As she settled onto the bareback pad she studied the guy's handsome face while considering her next move, wondering if she'd ever seen him before. After all, she had lived here all her life, and she knew just about everyone in these parts.

The guy definitely wasn't from around there, Lyssa decided. Twisting a lock of her hair, she debated pushing past him on Blue and seeing for herself what he was hiding. But then, glancing at her watch, she realized that Timorie was back at the ranch waiting for her jumping lesson in the indoor arena. Reluctantly she gathered Blue's reins.

"You're lucky I've got to skedaddle anyway," she said to the guy, opening Blue's right rein and bringing her leg back so that he would turn on his haunches.

"And don't come back!" the guy yelled as Lyssa and Blue started off.

Security guard or not, who does this big bully think he is? Lyssa couldn't help it. Laughter bubbled in her throat. Twisting around on the bareback pad, she called out, "You're going to have to work on your big, bad scary act. I'm not exactly shaking in my moccasins!"

The guy glared and quickly disappeared behind the building.

Lyssa furrowed her brow as she turned back around. *This is way too weird*, she thought. She and Blue walked slowly across the campus and made their way up to the frontage road. As the snow began falling more heavily, she brushed a few flakes from her face and blew out her breath.

"We ought to just forget about Timorie and charge back there," Lyssa murmured to her horse, stopping to gaze at the schoolyard one last time. "This snowfall is going to blot out the prints, and I'll never figure out what's going on here."

But she knew that it would be totally unfair to leave Timorie hanging, especially since she'd taken the trouble to get out to Black Thunder Ranch in spite of the bad weather. Sighing with disappointment, Lyssa studied the sky for a while, gazing at the snowflakes that were falling more swiftly and closer together. Shivering in spite of her layers of insulated clothing, Lyssa bit her lip.

"Oh, well," she muttered. "Let's get on home, Blue. I'll give you a nice armful of hay, and you can munch down some HorsePower so you'll be revved up for tomorrow. We're going to come back here and see if we can't get to the bottom of this."

Blue tossed his head, eagerly awaiting Lyssa's signal to trot. Patting his neck, Lyssa squeezed her heels, and she and Blue set off at a fast clip toward Black Thunder Ranch. When they hit a straightaway, she leaned low, letting Blue take the bit in his teeth. The wind burned her face as the two raced along the path, but the earlier magic she had felt when she first set out was gone. Instead she found herself puzzling over the mysterious horse and the agitated guy as she brought Blue back and slowed him to a walk for the final stretch home.

Rats, she thought, leaning over to undo the baling-wire loop at the gate of the main corral. *Just when I get my chance to tear up the powder, some stupid guy has to wreck it.*

Once Lyssa was inside the barn, she jumped down from Blue's back, unbuckling the girth holding the bareback pad in place. Steam rose from Blue as she pulled off the pad, and she turned it upside down on the tractor seat so that it would dry. As she did so she saw a note that Mitch had stuck under the barn phone: *Timorie canceled lesson. Rescheduled for tomorrow morning.*

"Great," Lyssa muttered. "So I came back here and blew my opportunity to nab that horse for nothing!"

Frustrated, Lyssa crumpled the note. Then she became aware of the piles of tack laid neatly across the hood of the tractor. Guiltily she surveyed the equipment that Mitch had finished cleaning and oiling.

And to top things off, I owe Mitch for finishing up without me, Lyssa thought as she set to work drying the sweaty area on Blue's back and rubbing him down thoroughly with a soft cloth. After brushing him, Lyssa applied some baby oil to Blue's muzzle to prevent the skin chapping that could be caused by the bitterly cold weather. Leaning down, she picked out his hooves, checking to be sure he hadn't sustained any cuts around the fetlock area from ice they might have traveled over.

Standing back, Lyssa surveyed her handiwork. When she was satisfied that her grooming session was complete, she put on Blue's thick winter blanket, buckling the surcingle securely.

"There you go," she murmured lovingly to her

horse. "You're all ready for dinner and a doze session in your nice warm house."

Blue tossed his head as Lyssa led him into his stall. After she fluffed the shavings, she kissed him good night on his nose, then turned out the lights and headed for the house.

It was getting dark, and the snow falling thickly made it seem even darker. Lyssa's eyes were drawn to the bright lights emanating from the ranch house. At the kitchen door she could hear the voices of her parents and aunt and uncle. Uncle Cal and Aunt Gwen had their own home set back behind the main house, near the men's bunkhouse, where Mitch lived, but often the two couples combined cooking duties and served up supper in Lyssa's house. Lyssa was crazy about her aunt and uncle, so it was an arrangement that suited her just fine.

Tonight, Lyssa saw as she stepped into the kitchen, Mitch was there as well. He was sitting on the linoleum floor across from Aunt Gwen, playing with the puppy, who was romping back and forth between them.

"Hi, everyone," greeted Lyssa, peeling off her parka and goose-down vest. Kicking off her lined moccasins, she shoved her feet into dry sheepskin slippers that were waiting by the kitchen door.

Her dad and Uncle Cal looked up from the stove, where they were spooning tamale casserole onto their plates. Mrs. Hynde was pouring milk into glasses at the table.

"We were about to start eating without you," her father said matter-of-factly. "Did you lose your way home?"

Lyssa snorted at the very idea of getting lost and walked over to pet the puppy. "Sorry I was late," she replied, crouching down. "Blue and I were having such a good time romping through the snow, I just kind of forgot the time."

"I noticed," Mitch exclaimed pointedly, leaning over to punch Lyssa playfully on the shoulder. "I oiled and oiled, and before I knew it, I was done with *our* project."

"Thanks for finishing up the tack for me, Mitch," Lyssa said as the puppy leaped up and placed his huge paws on her shoulders, causing her to fall over. "I'll make it up to you."

"Cool," Mitch said, grinning wickedly. "I've got a saddle you can repair, and Cody needs his mane thinned. While you're at it, he could use a couple of trailering and loading sessions, and then I'll think of some other things I need you to do for me."

"Ha ha," Lyssa replied, trying to fend off the eager puppy, who was now licking her ear lavishly. "You're so funny, I'm rolling on the floor laughing."

"No, you're rolling on the floor because Señor Grande knocked you over," quipped Mitch.

Glancing at the puppy, Lyssa swallowed hard. "Was this guy okay this afternoon?" she asked her mom when she sat up, wiping her wet ear. In the excitement of the afternoon, Lyssa realized she hadn't thought about the puppy at all. Her mom was busy enough working on the ranch accounts without having to take on the added responsibility of a needy new animal.

"Oh, yes," Mrs. Hynde said, looking over while the puppy flopped back down on the saddle blanket in front of the fire. "He kept me company while I did the books. He's going to be a great companion."

"Good," Lyssa said.

Whew. At least I don't have to worry about the puppy, she thought. *He seems to be fitting in here just fine.*

That just left worrying about the mysterious hoofprints and wondering what was up with the strange guy at the schoolyard, she decided, walking over to load up her plate for supper. After an afternoon of hard riding, Lyssa realized she was ravenous, and her mom's tamale casserole made her mouth water. When they were all seated at the table, Lyssa darted a look at Mitch.

"So," she began conversationally. "Meeting anyone special at the dance tonight?"

Mitch's face flushed bright red. "Maybe, maybe not," he said evasively. "How about you? Who are you meeting?"

Lyssa wiggled her eyebrows. "Oh, I'm not about to lose my cool over anyone—unlike *some* people I know," she teased.

"Do you kids really think you ought to go out tonight?" Aunt Gwen asked with a touch of worry in her voice.

"They'll be fine," Lyssa's dad cut in. "The grange isn't that far from home."

Mitch grinned at Lyssa. "You're just jealous that you don't have someone to dance with except your goofy friends," he teased back.

Lyssa shot him a look. "Oh, I'm incredibly jealous," she said, her voice dripping with sarcasm. "It would be great to be getting all weirded out about some guy when I need to be concentrating on getting Blue ready for Rolex, now, wouldn't it?"

Turning to her dad, she switched the subject.

"Did you find the horses you were looking for this afternoon?" she asked.

Her dad's weathered face crinkled up in a smile. "Yep," he said. "Lindy and Ribbon took us up through section twelve, but we caught up with them before those rascals could go much farther."

"You didn't by any chance go near the high school, did you?" Lyssa asked, already knowing the answer. The ranch was divided into about twenty sections, and section twelve was in the opposite direction from the high school.

Rob Hynde shook his head as he took a forkful of casserole. "Nope," he said.

Mitch glanced over at Lyssa. "Why do you ask?"

Lyssa looked at her old friend, wishing she hadn't said anything. Once she mentioned the hoofprints, Mitch would start asking a zillion questions, and for some reason Lyssa didn't want to draw too much attention to her find. Something made her want to work things out on her own.

"It's no big deal," she said quietly, hoping no one would ask more questions.

Uncle Cal took a gulp of the scalding coffee he always drank at supper. "Speaking of snow, there is a lot of it," he said. "I wonder if we'll have as big a snow as last winter."

"Oh, Cal, don't be ridiculous," her aunt Gwen

replied. "That was a hundred-year storm. We won't see another like that for a long time to come."

Everyone's eyes traveled to the window at the same time, where the snow was falling steadily and piling up at the edge of the panes.

"All the cattle are in, as well as the horses, and everything's battened down," Lyssa's father said. "We don't have any dudes here to worry about. So, as they say, let it snow."

After dinner Lyssa sat in front of the fireplace, petting the puppy and gazing at the crackling flames, knowing she ought to get up and dig through her closet for something to wear to the dance. But she just couldn't muster the energy to move. Over and over she pictured the hoofprints, wondering just how they'd gotten there.

And the guy who shooed me away . . . what was up with that? she wondered, finding herself thinking against her will about how cute he was, even if he had acted like a complete dork in an effort to scare her off.

As Lyssa stared at the red and orange flames, she pictured the angular face of the young guy, remembering how his dark hair had curled behind his ear and how his green eyes had flashed with electricity.

Glancing over at Mitch, who was now putting on

his jacket, Lyssa thought back to how she'd once been so nervous and excited about him. She'd never felt like that about anyone else—till she met the strange guy at the schoolyard.

Don't be a bonehead! she told herself. *Of course you were nervous. You knew he was up to something, that's all.*

Mitch started rattling his keys as a hint that if she wanted a ride, she'd better get going.

"I'll just be a sec," Lyssa yelled, heading to her room and sighing as she stood in front of her closet. She really didn't feel like bothering to get dressed up, but her friends were expecting her. Finally Lyssa pulled on a blue sweater and a pair of black jeans. They would have to do. Quickly she braided her dark hair, securing it with a turquoise barrette.

Moments later she was seated in Mitch's truck, haphazardly applying some lip gloss with her finger.

"I see you're going all out to make yourself look good, but I'm afraid you'll need to do more than slap on a little lip gunk," Mitch teased.

"We can't all be naturally good-looking like you," Lyssa shot back. Then she giggled as she caught Mitch checking himself out in the rearview mirror. "That's the sixth time you've checked out your mug since we left the ranch. Whoever she is, she must be pretty special."

Mitch nodded and held up his hand in a gesture of

surrender. "Her name's Kelly, and yeah, actually she is special," he said seriously. "But no more teasing. Let's call a truce, just for this evening!"

Lyssa nodded and laughed. "Oh, all right. Just for tonight," she agreed reluctantly.

Once inside the dance hall, Lyssa quickly found her friends standing in a group by the big stone fireplace. They waved Lyssa over as soon as they saw her. As she made her way over to them she smiled, glad that she had come after all. It would be nice to laugh and joke with her friends and get her mind off the mysterious tracks for a while.

Just as Lyssa had pushed through the crowd and reached her friends, Gabriela ran up to her, towing along a thin guy who towered above Gabriela by several inches.

I can see why he's a basketball player, Lyssa thought.

"Lyssa, I want you to meet Brendan Littlefield," Gabriela cried.

"Nice to meet you," Lyssa responded. She shook hands with him.

"Lyssa's my eventing instructor," Gabriela said to Brendan. Then her face clouded. "That is, she *was*, till I had to send my horse away."

"That's too bad," Brendan said.

Gabriela shrugged. "Oh, I'm over it," she said quickly,

gazing into Brendan's eyes. "I guess I've outgrown horses, anyway. I've got other things on my mind now."

Lyssa looked over at her friend, shocked at what she had just heard. She stared after Gabriela as Brendan pulled her out on the dance floor.

What did that mean? she thought with amazement. *Doesn't Gabriela care about Mystic anymore?*

"I'm going to get some punch," she muttered to no one in particular. The punch table was across the room, and it took Lyssa several minutes to work her way through the crush of people. Waiting until the people in front of her had filled their cups, Lyssa finally had her turn at the punch bowl. Just as she lifted the ladle, she saw a good-looking guy walk up to the table. Lyssa's mouth dropped open. It was the guy who had tried to scare her away from the high school! He was wearing different clothes now, and his black cowboy hat was dressed up with a silver band. His shirt and jeans were pressed. Lyssa couldn't help noticing how the green in his shirt set off his eyes.

For a moment Lyssa just stared, the ladle dangling in her hand. Then she struggled to come up with something clever to say to mask her surprise.

"Ah, I see the security company gives their employees some much-needed time off," she said, locking eyes with him. She tried to keep her voice steady, but in truth, she found she was having trouble breathing. When she was finally able to suck in a breath, she detected a faint scent of lime.

The guy's face paled. "What are *you* doing here?" he asked, visibly shaken.

Lyssa looked pointedly at her cup. "It's called punch," she said, dipping the ladle into the punch bowl. "And I'm about to drink it."

"Want to dance instead?" he asked, jerking a thumb toward the floor, now crowded with couples slow-dancing.

"I usually don't slow-dance with strangers," Lyssa replied. But then her curiosity got the better of her. "Okay, but only if you promise you'll tell me what you're being so secretive about," she added, setting down her empty cup.

"I never make promises," he said, slipping his hand around her waist and leading her out onto the floor before she could protest.

"Who's this, Lyssa?" Gabriela asked as she and Brendan danced up next to them.

Lyssa shrugged. "Beats me. He lured me out here under false pretenses," she said, glaring at the guy. "He *claims* he's a security guard."

Gabriela mouthed, "Cute security guard," and she and Brendan moved away.

"Aha. So your name's Lyssa," the guy said, pulling her close to him. "I'm Tony. And fine—so maybe I'm not a security guard. But *you're* way too nosy."

Lyssa drew back, searching the guy's face. "Are you threatening me?" she asked.

Tony shook his head. "Actually, I'm not the threatening type," he murmured.

Lyssa leaned against his strong shoulder, trying to figure out her next move as she inhaled that amazingly pleasant scent of lime again. Under different circumstances she'd have liked to melt into him and forget about hoofprints—or anything else, for that matter. Tony sure was perplexing. "Well, you're the sneaking-around type, that's for sure."

"And you're a really nice girl who's better off not being mixed up in things she doesn't know about." Tony sighed. "Just forget you ever saw me, okay?" he pleaded.

With that, he suddenly pulled away and disappeared through the crowd, leaving Lyssa standing there wondering if she had dreamed the whole thing up.

Scowling, she walked off the dance floor, craning her neck as she looked around to see if she could spot Tony, but he was nowhere to be found.

What's up with him? Lyssa thought. *I wonder where he went, and why he came here in the first place. And if he wanted me to forget him, why did he dance with me?*

During the evening she asked a few of her former schoolmates if they knew who he might be, but no one had a clue. For a while Lyssa walked around the hall wondering if she might bump into him again, but with no success. She did catch an eyeful of Mitch, who looked as though he'd been surgically attached to a cute, athletic-looking red-haired girl. He danced with her dance after dance.

So that's Kelly, Lyssa thought. *He looks like he's completely flipped for her.*

She was happy for Mitch, but she wished she weren't so distracted and could just enjoy the evening instead of thinking about Tony and those hoofprints. She sat at a table with Amy and Kyla and a few others, drumming her fingers to the music and turning down several offers to dance, her thoughts miles away.

A while later Lyssa bummed a ride home with Mr. Lattimer, who, much to Gabriela's annoyance, was worrying about the weather so much that he decided to pick up Gabriela early.

Gabriela scowled in the back of the car. "I guess I just ought to be glad that my parents let me go in the first place," she whispered. "My mom made Dad tie the blizzard line from the house to the barn so he wouldn't lose his way in case there's a whiteout. Dumb, huh?"

Lyssa made a noncommittal noise. Stringing up a blizzard line was a common country practice. By holding on to the line, people could make their way between two buildings without losing their bearings. It was true, though, that people didn't usually string a blizzard line unless it looked like there was going to be a huge storm.

Gabriela leaned closer to Lyssa. "So what did you think of Brendan?" she asked, keeping her voice low so her dad wouldn't hear. Lyssa knew her parents didn't approve of Gabriela's dating yet.

"He seems like a sweetheart," Lyssa whispered back. But despite her smile, she was still annoyed at her friend for her weird comments about Mystic.

By the time Lyssa slipped into her house, she'd forgotten about Gabriela and returned to her puzzling thoughts. Who was Tony, really? Why had he been at the dance, where had he disappeared to, and what had he meant when he'd said she'd do better not to get mixed up in whatever he was up to?

She'd find out more the next day, she decided firmly. Snow or no snow, she was going to set out at first light and get some answers.

You just try to scare me off this time, Tony! Lyssa thought, her heart thumping with excitement.

5

"OKAY, TIMORIE," CALLED LYSSA. "TAKE THAT LINE AGAIN. And this time I want you to put in that eighth stride. You're rushing and trying to do it in seven, and poor Valmont here is really having to scramble to take that chicken coop."

It was early the next morning, and Lyssa was in the indoor arena on B.C., one of the ranch's oldest horses, giving Timorie Randall her jumping lesson. Lyssa was wearing her trusty Thinsulate parka, but even so, she could feel the cold wind cutting through the arena. Although it kept out the snow and ice, the arena—built by Lyssa's family with the help of the neighbors— wasn't completely weather-tight. Still, it had made all the difference to Lyssa and Blue's training schedule.

Normally Lyssa couldn't jump much during the winter. It was far too dangerous to take horses over jumps when it was icy. But with the addition of the large, sturdy building, everything had changed. Though she couldn't jump cross-country, at least she could practice her stadium jumping all winter long—and give lessons as well.

It was mornings like this when Lyssa really appreciated the indoor arena. So what if it was snowing like crazy outside? Inside the arena was dry—albeit cold and drafty. Lyssa had set up a simple course for Timorie, who had been taking lessons from Lyssa for several months. Sometimes it seemed to Lyssa that she was getting nowhere with the headstrong girl. Although Timorie was a natural rider who had a good seat and quiet hands, she was scatterbrained, and on lots of occasions she simply refused to listen.

She reminds me of me, Lyssa thought with amusement as, once again, the thin, blond-haired girl thundered down the line, leaving out the final stride. Lyssa shrugged and cupped her hands in front of her mouth.

"Come into the center," she called out, her voice echoing off the arena walls.

Timorie ducked her head and rode over. "Sorry," she muttered, pushing up her glasses. "I try to hold Valmont in, but he gets strong."

Lyssa tried to look stern, but she knew she wasn't

fooling Timorie. "You need to be the *itancan*," she said quietly, using the Native American word for leader. "Valmont needs to know that you're the leader, and then he'll respond."

Timorie nodded. "I know, I know," she mumbled. "It's just that sometimes being an *itancan* isn't easy."

"That's for sure," Lyssa replied with a laugh. "Blue reminds me of that all the time. But it's something to strive for if you want to be a better rider."

Glancing at her watch, Lyssa saw that the morning was slipping away. "Now cool down Val, and let's go put these hardworking guys away. We don't want to keep your mom waiting."

Timorie hated to end her lessons, and she dawdled on her way back to the barn. Lyssa, following slowly behind on B.C., gritted her teeth with impatience. She couldn't wait to tack up Blue and ride back to the school. Every minute she was delayed only made it less likely she'd find the mysterious horse!

"No, I'm sorry, pup, you can't come," Lyssa said a while later to the fawn puppy that was gamboling around at her feet. "You'd freeze your tail off out there. Your coat just isn't thick enough. And anyway, this is a horse-and-girl thing."

She was in the kitchen packing food and hot coffee in a Thermos in preparation for her ride. Stashing everything she could think of into a leather saddlebag, Lyssa stepped around the pup, trying not to feel guilty for leaving him behind. Like most dogs, Lyssa knew, this guy would love to run along the trails while she rode, sniffing in the snow and chasing any wildlife that he happened to find. But he was too young to run the miles she expected to cover today. And he was too new. He'd get lost in no time. There would be time in the spring to introduce the puppy to the great outdoors, when the weather had warmed up.

"Fruit slices, granola bars, and Aunt Gwen's famous apple-cinnamon muffins. That ought to do it," she murmured, fastening the straps on the saddlebag and tossing it over her shoulder. She shoved a small flashlight in her pocket and, as an afterthought, her woolly cap, just in case.

Kneeling down, she rubbed the puppy's soft ears. "I'll be gone for a few hours," she said gently. "So you stay warm in here and keep Mom and Aunt Gwen outta trouble. When I get back, we'll play awhile, and by then I might even have thought up a good name for you. How about that?"

Trying to block out the sound of the puppy's whining as she stepped out into the arctic air, Lyssa made her way down to the barn. There were large drifts at the bases of the fence posts and along the perimeter of the building.

"I wish it hadn't snowed again. How will I ever find that horse?" she groaned softly, looking around.

Sighing as she entered the warmth of the barn, Lyssa inhaled the sweet smell of hay and horse. Blue whinnied and pawed in his stall, impatient to be off.

"I'm coming, sweetie," she called, setting the saddlebag on the tractor seat.

Leading Blue out to the center of the barn, Lyssa groomed him carefully. While she picked out his feet she told him about her plans to resume tracking the horse. "We'll go back to the schoolyard and have a good look around," she said into his flicking ear. "And if Tony is there, we'll tell him to back off, and we'll look anyway."

Blue snorted as if in agreement.

"And today, for once, you're going to wear a saddle," she explained. "I know you don't like saddles much, but I need something to lash a few provisions onto. We might be out all day, and I don't want to have to turn back just because either of us gets hungry. We *have* to find the horse that's making those tracks! Don't you agree, Blue?"

Lyssa could tell that her horse was eager to go. He danced around while she saddled him up with her oldest eventing saddle, even though she frowned at him and told him to mind his ground manners. He stretched his head down and forward, yawning to take the snaffle. Turning to watch Lyssa with ears pricked as she tied on the saddlebag, Blue let out a low, throaty whicker. Clearly he was eager to set off.

"Let's go," Lyssa said, leading him out of the barn into the main corral. There she mounted, zipping up her parka against the cold and pointing Blue in the direction of the high school.

As Lyssa rode along, she glanced at the jagged, snow-clad peaks ahead of her. They were so beautiful and regal, they made Lyssa catch her breath. Nearing the school, Lyssa began studying the trail intently, looking for any fresh hoofprints, but she didn't see anything besides an expanse of unmarred snow.

"We have to be quiet this time, big guy," Lyssa whispered, leaning low over her horse's shoulder. "We don't want to give any advance warning to Tony that we're coming. I'm going to have a look in that shed if it kills me!"

Making her way over to the locker room area, Lyssa dismounted and led Blue along the wall toward the equipment shed. As she approached the door she saw that the snow was striated, and from the looks of it, the marks were fresh.

"Weird," Lyssa muttered softly, her eyes darting around to see if anyone was watching her.

Straightening, she saw that the lock on the equipment shed was broken. The door was standing slightly ajar. She turned to Blue.

"Stand," she said to her horse, pulling his reins over his head. Years earlier she had trained Blue not to move until she gave the signal. "I'll be back in a sec."

Tentatively Lyssa pushed open the door, wincing at how loudly it creaked. Stepping inside the darkened interior, Lyssa could see nothing. She reached into her pocket and pulled out her flashlight, flicking it on and scanning the shed with its tiny beam. At first she saw nothing but sports equipment, chalk buckets, and benches stacked floor to ceiling. But then the tiny beam shone on several wisps of hay.

Lyssa sucked in her breath as she saw a fresh pile of manure in the corner. Obviously a horse had been here—and recently!

"And that means good old Tony was hiding it!" she exclaimed triumphantly, walking back out of the shed to take Blue's reins. "I *knew* he was up to no good."

She led Blue away from the shed, studying the snow markings in the doorway again. "They're definitely not natural," Lyssa mused. "Someone made them with a rake or a broom or something. Someone who didn't want to be tracked."

Lyssa could feel her heart pounding as she inched along the building toward the back. It started beating even faster when, a few yards away, Lyssa spotted a trail of fresh hoofprints leading away from the schoolyard, past the fields, and off toward the mountains.

"This way, Blue," she said, running back to her horse, her excitement making her voice tremble.

Mounting hurriedly, she clucked, urging Blue forward.

"We're going to find our mystery horse any minute, I just know it," Lyssa called out, turning him in the direction of the hoofprints The two of them moved slowly across the fields and down a slight ravine. The hoofprints would disappear every few minutes, and Lyssa guessed it was because clumps of snow had fallen from overhead branches, obliterating the small indentations. But then they reappeared, making their way steadily westward. Soon Lyssa realized they were beginning the ascent to the Beartooth Mountains.

What is that crazy guy thinking? Lyssa wondered. Riding along the flatlands in the snow was one thing. Taking to the mountains on horseback was another thing altogether.

You're heading into avalanche country, Tony, Lyssa thought grimly.

As long as Lyssa could remember, she had been warned to stay away from the mountains during the winter months. After all, it didn't take much to unleash an avalanche. A few days of snow, some wind, and some temperature fluctuations could all create one of nature's more terrifying demonstrations of power.

Though avalanche forecasters were getting better at reading the terrain and predicting susceptible areas, Lyssa knew forecasting wasn't an exact science. Snowboarders and snowmobilers triggered avalanches all the time. Disregarding warnings to stay away from the backcountry, they would heedlessly take to the slopes. Before they knew it, they would hear a *whoosh* and be buried under acres of snow. Some would be swept helplessly off a cliff with the force of a class-five rapid. Some of the victims carried avalanche beacons, which helped the snow patrol locate them. Other times the snow patrol had to use probes. And still the bodies often weren't discovered for weeks.

"We're dealing with a newbie here, Blue—or else a real brain-dead type," Lyssa said with disgust. "I guess we'd better forget tracking any further."

But as she sat back in her saddle and studied the mountains, she couldn't help feeling that maybe it was

71

her duty to try to help the mysterious horse—to save it from the consequences of Tony's ignorance. She'd feel terrible later if she found out he and the horse had been trapped in the mountains and she hadn't tried to help.

"It's probably the stupidest thing I've ever done," Lyssa muttered to Blue. "But I guess I ought to follow them—if only to save their fool hides."

As the ground began to rise beneath her, Lyssa was torn between wanting to tear up the trail quickly and taking it slowly. If she and Blue could gather some momentum, perhaps they could catch up with their quarry before they got too far. On the other hand, she had to ride slowly enough to be able to track.

What would I do if I were trying to throw someone off? Lyssa asked herself. *Get off the main trail and cut across some switchbacks, of course!*

That decided it. She would go slowly and be on the lookout for the slightest signs that Tony was zigzagging and trying to throw them off.

After riding for an hour, Lyssa stopped briefly, lifting her chin and inhaling the cold air to see if she could detect the scent in the air that would tell her whether or not it was about to snow again.

"Yup. But it just doesn't matter," Lyssa said, reaching down to pat Blue's shoulder. "We've got to keep going."

She sat still on Blue's back, wondering if Tony was riding the horse, and deciding that he must be. After all, there were no shoe prints that she could see. But what if he was hiding his prints? And if so, why would he be trying so hard not to be detected?

"This is making me crazy," Lyssa muttered aloud.

Mentally she ran through the list of possible reasons someone would hide a horse in the shed at the high school and then head toward the mountains on a snowy day.

One: Tony lost his horse, found him again, and now is heading home, which happens to be near the base of the mountains, Lyssa thought. But as she formed the idea, she knew how far-fetched it was.

Two: Tony found a lost horse and is returning it to the owner. She shook her head. If this were the case, he wouldn't have acted so strangely when she ran into him at the equipment shed. And at the dance he wouldn't have told her she was nosy.

No, she decided. She was back to square one.

Too bad, she decided, clucking to Blue as she once again pictured Tony's flashing green eyes. *He's an awfully cute bad guy.*

Blue shook himself and they set off once again, heading into what her father called Wildcat Canyon. As they rode alongside the creek that ran down the center, Lyssa spotted a long stretch of tracks ahead of them. Knowing that the horse wouldn't be able to suddenly change directions because the creek formed a barrier, Lyssa decided she could safely let Blue gallop for a while.

As she cued him, closing her legs and letting the reins run through her fingers, Blue responded eagerly, practically shooting out from beneath her. Listening to the thuds of his rapid footfalls, Lyssa felt adrenaline surge through her body. Closing her eyes, she imagined she was on the cross-country course at Rolex, the big four-star event held at Lexington Horse Park in April. Blue had just burst out of the starting box, and they were making their approach to the first big fence.

Without thinking, Lyssa let out a resounding whoop that careened back and forth between the walls of the canyon. Instantly she regretted it. After all, though Tony evidently thought he might be followed, there was no need to give away her exact position.

"I can't believe I did such a boneheaded thing," Lyssa scolded herself. "Now Tony knows there's someone behind him." Reluctantly she slowed Blue and stopped to dig out the snow and ice packed in the soles of his hooves.

When they had gone several more miles, Lyssa dismounted, loosening Blue's girth and shaking the kinks out of her legs. The hoofprints stood out more than ever, and Lyssa smiled.

Her smile began to fade as the fat snowflakes that had been meandering from the sky started falling more rapidly. Snowflakes settled on Lyssa's eyelashes, and a slight wind began blowing, causing the snow to fall at a slant.

Good-bye, tracks! Just as we were making real progress, Lyssa thought mournfully as she remounted. Within minutes the tracks disappeared, and Lyssa stopped midtrail and let out a deep sigh.

"I guess we have to face it," she muttered dejectedly to Blue, brushing snow from his mane. "Time to head home."

But just as Lyssa started to gather her reins, she heard a shrill whinny that echoed off the canyon walls. Though the snow muffled the sound quickly, Lyssa could tell that the whinny had come from nearby.

Blue's head snapped up, muscles tense, ears pricked.

"Did you hear how close that was? Forget what I said about going home," Lyssa said, tilting her head. "What's a little snow? We're closing in on our mystery horse!"

6

"I COULD HAVE SWORN THE SOUND CAME FROM UP THERE," Lyssa said, looking up at a bank rising from the trail. "But what if it bounced around from somewhere else?"

Biting her lip for a moment, Lyssa hesitated. The last thing she wanted to do was go completely off the trail, especially if she wasn't sure which way to go. The snowdrifts around her were huge, and there was no telling what lay hidden underneath them. Gullies, sharp rocks, or animal burrows were just a few of the unpleasant surprises she might find if she stepped off the trail.

Finally she sent up a quick prayer, closed her legs, and urged Blue up the bank. The big horse plunged and scrambled upward through the snow, which was almost chest-high in some places. Twice he got tangled up in some snow-covered undergrowth but quickly worked his way out of it. Finally they reached the top.

Lyssa looked around quickly, seeing nothing. For a few moments she sat still in her saddle, straining to hear a snap of a twig, a crunch of snow, or anything else that might signal just where the horse was.

"Maybe we went the wrong way after all," she whispered into Blue's flicking ear.

She rode back and forth, trying to decide whether she should shoot back down the bank or remain up there, where at least she had a better vantage point. From this position she could see much farther than before.

Suddenly she heard the whinny again. This time the sound seemed to come clearly from her left, past a clump of pines. Lyssa didn't hesitate. She turned Blue's head toward the sound, squeezing his sides. When they reached a flat expanse, she cued Blue into an extended trot while she scanned both sides of the snowy path, sure that any second she would spot the horse they had been following. For a fraction of a second she reveled in the sensation of Blue's animated yet smooth gait. But then she jerked herself back to her mission and began focusing intently on the ground, hoping she'd find hoofprints that would tell her exactly where to go.

Finally she saw them: the distinct rounded shapes that had started this whole adventure in the first place.

"Check it out, Blue," Lyssa whispered with excitement. "Look at the pattern of the footfalls. The back hooves are overreaching the front hooves. That horse is trotting, too. Seems like Tony is in a hurry. He's trying his hardest to get away from us."

Higher and higher horse and rider climbed, Lyssa's nerves vibrating as her eyes swept every inch of the snowy terrain that bordered the trail.

"See this, big guy?" Lyssa whispered, pausing to study several broken branches. "They've come right through here, and these breaks are fresh. We're practically on top of them. I just know it."

Leaning forward, Lyssa could smell the sharp scent of newly exposed wood and sap.

"This happened just seconds ago," Lyssa whispered, her heart beginning to pound again.

The snow was now falling so heavily, Lyssa was beginning to have trouble seeing ahead. She jammed on her woolly hat and brushed at her face impatiently, wishing she'd brought goggles.

Well, I can't think of everything, she told herself, blinking rapidly and scrunching up her face.

The ground was rising sharply, and the wind began howling. Every one of Lyssa's senses told her to turn back, but she urged Blue forward for a few more yards.

"This is nuts," she admitted, her teeth beginning to chatter. "Maybe we ought to duck under an overhang and wait this out."

Suddenly Lyssa considered the possibility that Tony might have gotten the same idea. Even now, she thought, he might be overhead somewhere, standing next to the mysterious horse and watching her as she and Blue continued up the trail. Lyssa lifted her head as she rode, trying to spot any caves or overhangs where he might take shelter. Glancing around her at the steeply rising canyon walls, she half expected to see green eyes staring back.

"Kinda creeps you out, doesn't it, big guy?" she whispered to her horse, trying to calm herself.

Where could he hide out? she thought. *Of course!* Roger's Ridge was around here somewhere. One summer Lyssa had camped under the overhang with her family. Her father had named it in honor of his brother, who had discovered the overhang when they were boys.

As Lyssa continued looking upward, trying to pinpoint the ridge, she sucked in her breath at the sight of the tall mountains looming on both sides of the canyon. Their flanks were covered with unbroken walls of snow, and they looked daunting and immense.

Without thinking, Lyssa stopped Blue and closed her hands on the reins slightly as she sat deep in her seat, gazing in wonder at the steep, slab-covered slopes. Blue backed abruptly, stopping only when he stepped off the trail and bumped into a tree behind them.

I can't believe I did that, Lyssa thought as she felt Blue's haunches make contact with the tree trunk. Then she heard a *whoosh*. Reacting instinctively, she dug her heels into Blue's sides so that he shot forward the instant the tree dumped its heavy load of snow, which cascaded down a slope right next to them. Blue spooked, leaping sideways, then whirling to meet his enemy in a primal reaction to the sudden sound. As he did so, his shoulders brushed against a sapling, snapping it in such a way that the sound it produced was like a rifle shot.

"Easy there, Blue," Lyssa called frantically, struggling to control the frightened horse, who began plunging wildly. "I'm here with you. Everything's going to be all right."

Lyssa applied a pulley rein and fought to bend Blue around her leg, crooning in his ear the whole time, "It's okay. It's okay." She hated using the pulley rein, knowing how hard it was on Blue's soft mouth, but there wasn't any choice. If he bolted, chances were he'd slip and fall right over the edge of the steep trail.

A few seconds later Blue stopped plunging, but Lyssa continued to turn him in circles till she felt sure his panic had passed. Finally she was so dizzy, she had to stop. For a few moments she breathed in deep gulps of the frigid air, trying to slow down her wildly tattooing heart.

Whoa. That was close, Lyssa thought.

She continued sucking in air while she patted Blue's trembling neck and wondered just what she should do.

But just as she was considering whether to continue up the trail or not, she heard a strange *whoomp* sound and saw several small cracks radiating from beneath Blue's hooves. The next second, Lyssa felt the earth trembling.

"What is going on?" Lyssa cried out, looking up at the steeply sloping walls of Wildcat Canyon.

It was then that she saw a huge slab of snow break away, falling as if in slow motion. For an instant Lyssa stared, mesmerized, before it suddenly registered in her brain what she was seeing.

"Avalanche!" Lyssa cried out, turning Blue's head.

There was no time to waste!

Quickly she squeezed her heels at his sides, and she and Blue tore off at a terrifying pace down the steep trail. Rocking forward, Lyssa leaned close to his shoulder. The snow and wind whipped at her face, sending tears down her cheeks that froze instantly. Frantically Lyssa brushed at her face to loosen the ice, all the while feeling herself being flung from side to side in the saddle as Blue negotiated the twists and turns of the trail.

"You can do it, Blue," Lyssa called to her horse as she struggled to maintain her seat. Adrenaline surged through her, and she fought to control her panic as she considered the possibility that the avalanche might be right behind them. If so, there was no way, no matter how fast Blue was, that he could outrun it.

Lyssa had never seen an avalanche before, except on TV, but she knew that they were devastatingly fast, unstoppable juggernauts that would wipe out anything in their path, burying everything under tons of snow. Galloping on grimly, Lyssa tried to blot out the thought that any second she and Blue would be swept down the mountainside and off a cliff in a rushing torrent of white.

Flashing back to the avalanche segment she'd seen on TV, Lyssa pictured the search-and-rescue team using their avalanche transceivers to try to locate the bodies of several snowmobilers who had accidentally released a huge avalanche near a snow-packed cirque. She had horrifying visions of snow patrollers traversing the avalanche path searching for her body and Blue's.

Maybe they'd use search-and-rescue dogs to try to locate them.

Stop it! Lyssa commanded herself, pressing herself even more onto Blue's shoulder and forcing herself to look ahead. She felt the raw power of his body as he thundered on, his neck stretched out ahead of him, his ears flattened.

Just ahead Lyssa spotted a huge tree trunk that had fallen across the trail. From where she stood, it looked to be at least five feet high. She was approaching it from uphill, and she had no way of knowing what the drop would be like on the other side. Darting a glance to either side, Lyssa realized that there was no choice. She and Blue would have to take their chances and jump it.

"It's no bigger than anything we'll see at Rolex," Lyssa muttered, summoning her last ounce of courage.

Gathering up her reins slightly, Lyssa slowed Blue just a fraction as she centered the big horse.

Heaven only knows what's on the other side. Oh, well. Here goes nothing! she thought as Blue gathered himself for a mighty takeoff. Lyssa felt her heart jump in her throat as he shot into the air, and she clung tightly, throwing herself forward and giving him enough rein for a huge effort.

When they landed, Lyssa gasped at the impact,

wincing at the thought of the pounding Blue's feet and knees were taking. But she didn't dare stop. She could feel and hear the snow rushing down the mountain, and she had no idea how close it was.

Scanning her memory banks for anything more that she'd ever seen or read about avalanches, Lyssa suddenly remembered a documentary she'd seen in middle school about an early American explorer who'd been caught in an avalanche. He'd managed to save himself by swimming a sort of backstroke to keep from being sucked into the depths of the snow.

If I get caught, I'll just have to swim like that, Lyssa thought desperately. *But what about Blue?*

As Blue plunged down the mountain bravely, Lyssa hung on for dear life, her leg muscles locking and cramping. Gritting her teeth against the pain, Lyssa found herself considering a new fear: The avalanche was heading in the direction of the ranch. If it was big enough—and judging from the deafening rumble behind her, it seemed to be—it would cut a catastrophic swath right through the ranch.

"Oh, no," Lyssa moaned, her physical pain now counting for nothing next to the paralyzing realization that her family and their animals could be wiped out in literally seconds. "Come on, Blue. Give it all you've got!" Lyssa yelled, the force of the sharp wind hitting her in the face and stuffing her words right back down her throat.

Blue galloped bravely on, and Lyssa wasn't sure if it was her heels dug into his sides or the incessant rumbling that was driving him on.

Daring to pause and look over her shoulder as she and Blue finally descended to the base of the mountain, Lyssa was horrified to see a white wall of snow that seemed to be hundreds of feet high crashing down the mountainside.

Once again she leaned low over Blue's rhythmically pumping shoulder and sent him hurtling toward home.

"There's no way we can make it in time," Lyssa mumbled, her teeth chattering. "Well, if I have to die trying to warn my family, so be it!" she added grimly.

The rumble seemed to come closer and closer, but Lyssa's gaze was now locked on the faint light of the ranch house she could see in the distance.

Any minute now, she thought with a strange kind of acceptance, *Blue and I are going to be swept up.*

Finally Lyssa summoned the courage to look over her shoulder again, and in one magnificent moment she saw the tumbling wall of snow shift direction sharply to the right and cascade wildly through a smaller canyon that led to a flat expanse where her neighbors, the Johnsons, had their summer pasture. At this time of year the pasture was empty, since all the horses and cattle had been brought to the lower pastures months ago.

It took a few seconds before Lyssa was able to think straight, and she galloped on, her eyes riveted to the dreadful beauty of the dramatic scene.

"We're saved!" shouted Lyssa, turning around and throwing her fist in the air in a gesture of triumph. Quickly she brought Blue down to a gentle lope, then gradually slowed him to a trot and finally to a walk. Dismounting, she winced at the sharp pain shooting through her legs as she made contact with the frozen ground. Gritting her teeth, Lyssa loosened Blue's girth and walked slowly the rest of the way home, too tired to do anything but put one foot in front of the other.

Biting her lip, Lyssa considered the possibility that Tony and the horse had gotten caught in the avalanche. Maybe right now they were buried under acres of snow. She swallowed hard, feeling as if someone had kicked her in the stomach.

Then it occurred to her that they had been ahead of her, somewhere above the avalanche.

Whew, she thought.

A new thought struck Lyssa: What if now they were trapped and unable to get down the mountain? If Tony was unfamiliar with the mountains, he wouldn't know the alternative trails he could take to get back down. In this kind of weather, he and the horse could be stuck there for days, freezing and starving.

When Lyssa saw her mom and dad rush out of the house, their faces gray with worry, she forgot everything else and raced up to them, falling into their open arms, sobbing and gasping for air.

7

"TALK TO ME," MRS. HYNDE SAID OVER AND OVER AS Lyssa's sobs gradually subsided. "Are you okay?"

"I'm okay," Lyssa managed to say. "I'm just so glad that nothing happened to you guys."

"We're fine, punkin," her dad cut in.

"The avalanche—did you hear it?" Lyssa asked.

"We sure did. We saw it, too," her dad said. He looked more closely at her. "We were going a mile a minute trying to figure out how to move the horses. But there would have been no way to get all the horses and cattle out in time. We're incredibly lucky it decided to take a detour before it got here."

You don't know how lucky, Lyssa thought as her knees slowly began to regain strength.

Just then Mitch pulled up in his truck and jumped out, slamming the door and running over to Lyssa.

"I was trying to second-guess where that monster was going to go and see if I could gather some of the cattle before it was too late," Mitch exclaimed, peering closely at Lyssa. "You weren't out in that mess, were you?"

Lyssa nodded and bit her lip, trying to control her sobbing.

"Storm surfing again, huh, Lyss?" he cracked, ruffling her hair.

She shook him off and scowled at him, then smiled weakly. "Yeah, I guess I was," she admitted.

"As long as you and Blue are okay, there's no harm done, now, is there?" Mrs. Hynde added.

At the mention of Blue's name, Lyssa whirled around and looked him over quickly. In all the tumult, she hadn't stopped to consider that her horse could have gotten hurt—really hurt—in their mad dash to outrace the avalanche.

Lyssa ran her hands down his legs, gingerly exploring every inch. To her relief, she could feel that they were firm and cool. By some miracle, Blue hadn't sustained any injuries.

Lyssa wiped her face as she straightened up, exhaling deeply.

"He's okay," she said.

"But he's going to get stiff if he just stands here while we have our little family reunion," Mr. Hynde pointed out. Prying the reins from Lyssa's hands, he started to lead the big horse to the barn.

"I can take care of him, Dad," Lyssa called out, but she was cold to the bone and shivering so much that her words sounded muddled.

Her dad waved his hand as he continued walking. "Nonsense," he called out.

"Let him put Blue away," her mom said gently. "We need to get you inside and plant you in front of the fireplace. Your face is almost blue from the cold, and I don't want you getting frostbitten."

With that, Mrs. Hynde herded Lyssa through the kitchen door and out of the bitterly cold afternoon air.

A few moments later Lyssa was seated on the stone hearth in front of a roaring fire, a cup of hot cocoa in her hand and the enormous puppy flopped in her lap. Distractedly Lyssa scratched his ears while she absorbed the warmth of the fire and the steaming brown liquid. Her head was still whirling from the events of the afternoon, and she could swear she still felt the rumble from the avalanche.

"We were going out of our minds when we couldn't

find you," Mrs. Hynde said gently as she settled into the sofa, holding her mug. "What went on out there?"

"I did the biggest bonehead thing ever," Lyssa confessed to her mom.

"You mean slipping out this morning and not telling us where you were going?" Mrs. Hynde asked, arching one eyebrow. "I must admit, that was rather boneheaded."

Lyssa ducked her head guiltily. "Not that," she muttered. "It was after that. I—I was the one who triggered that avalanche. I've never seen anything like it. The sound was horrible. I raced home to try to warn you guys, but luckily it turned and shot down the gorge, where it wouldn't hurt anyone."

Mrs. Hynde sat up and blinked. "You set off that avalanche? How? Where were you?"

Lyssa looked down at the braided rug at her feet so that she wouldn't have to meet her mother's eyes. "I was up in the mountains by Roger's Ridge," she said unhappily.

"Roger's Ridge? What on earth for? In the middle of a snowstorm? You *know* better than that!"

Lyssa nodded. "But I *had* to!" she exclaimed. "I'd been following these hoofprints, and they led right up the mountain. I was just about to turn back when I heard a whinny, plain as day, from right nearby. So I had to keep going. Only I backed Blue into a tree and set off the avalanche, and here I am."

"I don't believe this!" Mrs. Hynde said, shaking her head. "You risked your life—and Blue's—over a set of *hoofprints?*"

"These aren't just any hoofprints," Lyssa interjected. "Maybe they belong to one of those missing horses I saw on the bulletin board at Beartooth Feed and Seed or something."

"This weather is too dangerous for you to be out helping round up missing horses," Mrs. Hynde replied. "We have the sheriff and other authorities to worry about that."

Lyssa looked away. She considered telling her mom about the encounter at the schoolyard with the mysterious guy, but something stopped her. She had a bad feeling her mom would probably think it was time to call some official. And Lyssa wanted to find the horse herself.

I've tracked that horse this long, she thought fiercely. *I've got to see it through.*

Lyssa sat up, clutching her blanket tightly around her. *I've got to get back there before it's too late!* she thought.

Mrs. Hynde stood and walked over to the kitchen.

"I'm going to heat up some beef stew for you. You're staying inside for the rest of the day! Mitch can do your evening chores for you."

Lyssa almost jumped up, unable to bear the thought of owing Mitch for anything else, but then thought better of it. She didn't want her mom to suspect she was already plotting to get back to the mountains.

"Okay," she said meekly as she continued scratching the puppy, her head whirling with plans to set out again the following morning. There was no way she could sit there all snug and warm while Tony and some horse were out there in the cold—possibly in grave danger. She had to change the subject, and quickly, before she got direct orders not to leave the ranch.

Looking at the puppy now sleeping peacefully in her lap, she called out to her mom, "So what should we name this guy?"

"How about Trouble?" Mrs. Hynde answered. "He chewed up your dad's lariat and two of my dish towels right after breakfast. Then he chased Aunt Gwen's cat all over the house, and now Mouser is hiding under the bed in the guest room."

"Oh, I'm sorry," Lyssa said, feeling guilty that not only had she caused her parents enough worry to last a lifetime, but on top of that, she had brought home a rambunctious puppy to make more work and stir things up. That was definitely the last thing her parents needed.

"Oh, it's no problem, really," Mrs. Hynde answered. "I was letting off steam, that's all. He's just young and playful. I was actually thinking we ought to call him Duke."

Lyssa grinned. "That's a great name, Mom," she said, finishing off her hot cocoa and carefully moving the sleeping puppy so she could stand up. "And now I think I'll drag myself into a hot bath. Every muscle in my body aches."

"Good idea. Then come down for your stew," her mom said.

After Lyssa had soaked for a long time in the tub, she put on her thick bathrobe and flopped on her bed, intending to doze for a few minutes.

But when she awoke and looked at her digital clock glowing in the dark, she saw that it was five o'clock in the morning.

I slept all night! I've got to get going! Lyssa thought, jumping up and changing into her flannel-lined jeans and a heavy woolen sweater. She'd have to be careful not to wake anyone. The last thing she wanted was for her parents to forbid her to make one last attempt at finding the source of the mysterious hoofprints.

Carrying her spare boots and padding into the darkened kitchen in her stocking feet, Lyssa quietly grabbed some granola bars for breakfast. The food she'd packed the day before would still be in the saddlebag, tied securely to her saddle. Sucking in her breath, she heated some soup she found in the refrigerator, snatching it from the flame the second it started bubbling. Quietly she filled the Thermos and screwed on the top. Walking over to the peg, Lyssa patted the pockets of her parka and felt the outlines of the can of nonstick spray, her flashlight, and Mrs. Lattimer's cell phone. The parka was still slightly damp, but it would have to do.

Moments later Lyssa jammed her feet into her boots and slipped out the kitchen door. Walking carefully so she didn't slip on the patches of ice on the path, she made her way over to the main corral. Lifting her gaze, Lyssa saw that it hadn't snowed any more during the night, and she smiled.

I'll be able to track more easily, she thought with satisfaction.

Blue's loud whinny, ordinarily a welcome sound, pierced the stillness of the predawn and sent a quick shiver of fear through Lyssa's heart. What if it woke up her dad or mom? Half expecting her parents to storm down to the barn at any minute, Lyssa stepped into the barn and ran over to Blue, hoping he would be quiet now.

After feeding Blue and checking him over thoroughly to make sure he was okay from his wild ride the day before, Lyssa saddled up and mounted. As Lyssa settled deep into her seat, Blue danced sideways.

He's nowhere near tired. He's as eager as I am! Lyssa thought.

"You've got heart, Blue, that's for sure," Lyssa murmured. "And I promise you, we are going to find that horse today."

She had just leaned over to lift the wire loop on the gate when she heard hoofbeats. Looking up, she saw Mitch riding toward her, mounted on his bay quarter horse, Cody.

"Morning," he said, grinning broadly at her. "And just where are you off to so early?"

Lyssa glared at Mitch. "None of your business!" she shot back.

Mitch took off his hat and scratched his head. "You aren't by any chance thinking of heading back into the hills, are you?"

"What if I am?" Lyssa asked, bristling. *Really*, she thought, *Mitch is carrying this big-brother thing a little too far!*

"You know you're out of your tiny mind," he said, his eyes piercing her. "Don't you think your parents would kick my butt if I let you ride out of here and right back into danger again?"

"Look, Mitch," Lyssa said pleadingly, "I know it's insane, but there's a guy up there and he's hiding a horse. And I've been tracking them for days. I've got to find them."

"Why would someone hide a horse in the mountains in this weather?"

Lyssa let out her breath in an explosive *whoosh*. "That's what I'm trying to find out."

Mitch put his hat back on and stared at Lyssa steadily. "Well, then, I'm coming with you."

Lyssa was horrified. "You can't," she said.

"Why not?"

Lyssa opened her mouth and closed it. She couldn't think of a single reason—other than pride. And actually, it might be nice to have another person along. What if she cornered Tony and it turned out he really was the threatening type? What if he tried to carry out his threats? He didn't seem violent, but there was no reason to take any more chances than she already had. She studied Mitch for a moment, wondering how much she should tell him.

Everything, she decided. She had always been able to trust Mitch.

"Fine, come if you must, " Lyssa muttered finally as she squeezed Blue's sides and turned toward the mountains. "But we've got to go quietly. He can't know that we're after him."

"Lyssa Hynde, I demand to know what you have gotten yourself tangled up in now," Mitch said sternly, following her.

While they rode, Lyssa filled Mitch in on the events of the past few days, starting with finding the hoof-prints and bumping into Tony at the dance, and ending with her wild ride down the mountain.

Mitch listened carefully, taking in her words. "So that was the guy you were dancing with the other night?" he asked. "I wondered who he was. You think he's some sort of horse thief?"

Lyssa nodded. "Maybe. Weird, huh?" she said.

"A dancing horse thief," Mitch mused. "Now I've heard everything. You sure know how to pick your dance partners," he added teasingly.

Lyssa frowned. "This is no time for joking," she snapped. "We've got to find him and get that horse!"

She clucked so that Blue moved ahead of Cody, and she and Mitch continued crossing the ranch. When the trail widened, they rode side by side.

"I'm freezing my butt off out here," Mitch complained.

"Yeah, maybe," agreed Lyssa. "But you've got to admit it's incredibly beautiful this time of the year."

"True," Mitch said, nodding. "Still, I could do without all the snow."

"Then move to Bermuda," she said, reaching over to flick his leg with the end of her reins.

"You said this was no time for joking, remember?"

Lyssa looked toward the mountains and smiled appreciatively. "Do you know that that Eskimos have more than two hundred and eighty words for snow?" she asked.

"I'm not surprised," Mitch commented dryly as Cody made his way through a knee-high snowdrift. "All I need are two: It sucks."

"Jamaica. That's another place you could move to," Lyssa tossed back.

"You're the biggest pain, you know that?" Mitch growled playfully.

When they got to the foothills, they stopped to let the horses drink from a small creek that ran alongside the trail. Making his way gingerly to the edge of the creek, Blue pawed at the frigid water, then raised his head, water dripping from his muzzle. Lyssa jumped off his back and wiped his mouth quickly. She didn't want ice forming and irritating his delicate skin.

"It's hard to imagine right now, but this spring

when the snows melt, this little creek is going to be roaring," Mitch mused while he checked Cody's feet for snow balling.

"Yeah, it would be nice to see it, but I hope I'll be in Kentucky by then," Lyssa said dreamily. "At Rolex."

"Oh, you will be," Mitch replied. "That is, if both of us don't turn into ice sculptures out here or you don't break your fool neck chasing after this phantom horse of yours."

"I have no intention of breaking anything," Lyssa said crisply, scanning the trail ahead for a fork that would lead away from the avalanche path.

As they continued climbing, Lyssa steered her horse along a trail that was parallel to the one she'd taken the day before. Mitch and Lyssa rode steadily for a time, neither of them saying much.

"Check this out," Lyssa said to Mitch, pointing to the gorge where the avalanche had gone. Sticking out of the high snow piles were broken trees and giant logs. To Lyssa, they looked like toothpicks stuck carelessly every which way.

Mitch let out a low whistle. "Yikes," he murmured, studying the devastation. "You set all that off just by backing Blue into a tree?"

Lyssa gulped and nodded. "Yep. That could have

been us thrown around like toys," she said quietly, instantly reliving her wild ride.

"Good old Mother Nature," Mitch murmured. "Kinda makes you feel small sometimes, doesn't it?"

"You can say that again," Lyssa replied. "I can't believe that all it took was one little vibration, and *whomp*—all this. But I'm definitely going to be more careful this time."

Lyssa and Mitch rode quietly and chose their path accordingly, staying away from areas where the snow seemed to be packed precariously.

Soon they neared the place where she had set off the avalanche. Lyssa slowed Blue, her ears on alert, hoping that maybe she'd get lucky and hear a whinny. But the only sounds were the cries of a lone hawk circling in the sky and the tiny rustlings of woodland creatures searching for food in the snow-covered undergrowth.

"Let's pick it up here," Lyssa said, pointing above the avalanche line.

Mitch drew up beside her on Cody. "But I don't see any tracks or anything. What makes you think we're anywhere close?"

"Just a feeling, that's all," Lyssa said.

Mitch drew up beside her. "A feeling, huh? Come

on. Do you have any idea what you're doing?" he asked while Cody pawed at the snow.

Lyssa could feel her spirits plummet. "Not at this precise moment, maybe," she admitted. "But in general, yes. We've got to find that horse."

The strain of tracking the elusive horse over the last couple of days was beginning to catch up with her. For the first time in a long time, she felt achy and bone tired.

If I'm tired, imagine how tired Blue must be, she thought with a flash of guilt. Looking down, she saw him moving patiently along, his stride smooth and even. *I hope I'm not pushing him too much.*

After all, Lyssa considered, swallowing hard, she was training him to be an Olympic eventing horse. She was supposed to be putting together a program of well-thought-out fitness gallops, interval training, jumping, and dressage sessions. She was *not* supposed to be risking injuring him just to chase after strange horses.

"Let's turn back," Mitch urged.

Lyssa shook her head. "You can turn back if you want," she replied irritably. Maybe she'd made a mistake agreeing to let Mitch come along. She didn't need him echoing her doubt.

Clucking softly and leaning forward, she cued Blue onward, Mitch shrugging and following on Cody.

"Come work at Black Thunder Ranch. It's not just a job—it's an adventure!" he joked as he caught up with Lyssa.

Lyssa grinned, glad now that Mitch had come along. Even though his jokes were pretty lame, at least he tried to lighten things up when he could. And it was comforting to have an almost-brother ride with her when she was trudging along for miles in the eerily silent and forbidding Montana mountains.

The sky stretched in an unending blanket of gunmetal gray, so it was hard to tell how late it was getting. Lyssa hadn't stopped to grab her watch before she left, so she only had a vague sense of how long they had been riding when suddenly Blue snorted and pricked his ears.

"Do you see what I see?" Mitch whispered, pointing to the trail.

Lyssa's heart thumped as she saw hoofprints crossing their path. "Cool! And look—these are boot prints!" she whispered. "Guess Tony's hoofing it for now!"

She and Mitch turned their horses, stepping off the trail to follow the prints.

Blue's nostrils flared as he arched his neck and began walking eagerly, resisting Lyssa's attempts to bring him back. She tried to steady him while she scanned the sides of the switchback, looking for broken twigs. Every so often her eyes would swivel back to the prints, boot prints mixed in with hoofprints.

"Why do you suppose Tony is walking?" Lyssa whispered.

"Giving his horse a rest?" Mitch whispered back.

Lyssa rolled her eyes. "Anyone concerned about that wouldn't have stolen a horse in the first place—nor brought him up to a place like this."

Mitch didn't answer.

"No fair, Blue," Lyssa whispered fiercely as her horse nickered. "You probably know right where that horse is. Why, oh, why can't I have a horse's sense of smell?"

Just then she heard a crackling in the brush up ahead.

We're closing in! Lyssa thought, squeezing Blue's sides.

Blue exploded forward, tearing headlong into a tangle of low branches. Lyssa ducked and shut her eyes, feeling the sting of springing branches smacking her in the face as Blue plunged on, zigzagging through the uneven terrain. Lyssa could hear Mitch and Cody behind them.

Suddenly Blue stopped so quickly, his hocks slid under him. Lyssa's eyes flew open as she fell forward up on his shoulder. Struggling to regain her seat, Lyssa at first didn't see the cause of Blue's abrupt halt. But then she saw Tony standing in the clearing, feet apart and arms crossed defiantly across his chest. "You again!" he exclaimed.

"That's right!" Lyssa retorted.

"I thought I told you to leave me alone!" Tony growled, glaring at her.

"Don't even start," Lyssa called out, holding up her hand. "This time I'm not going to be scared off by anything you say. I'm definitely not leaving till you show me the horse you've been hiding!"

8

"YOU CAN STAY HERE ALL DAY, THEN," TONY RETORTED. "But I'm not showing you any horse."

Lyssa slid off Blue, her eyes never leaving the guy. He looked nothing like the boy she'd seen the night of the dance. Now he was wearing torn jeans and a dirty duster. Dark hair shadowed his jawline, and his face was drawn with fatigue. Only his black hat was the same, though this time it didn't sport its silver band.

"Aha! So you admit you have a horse," Lyssa exclaimed, trying to stall for time while she figured out how to get past the guy and see what he was hiding.

"Yeah, I admit it," the guy said, making a shooing

motion. "Now turn around and go back where you came from."

Lyssa drew herself up to her full height and snorted. "Yeah, right," she said. "I've only been tracking you and this horse for days now, freezing my tail off and wearing out Blue here. You really think I'm going to turn back now and just forget I ever saw you?"

Tony switched to pleading. "Please, just go," he said. "None of this is your business."

He regarded Lyssa steadily, giving her a full dose of those shining green eyes. Then his eyes swept past her as Mitch and Cody rode into the clearing.

"Brought a friend, I see," he muttered.

Mitch glared at Tony, narrowing his eyes as he looked him over warily.

Lyssa tilted her head toward Mitch. "Mitch, meet Tony, our elusive horse thief," she said. "Tony, this is Mitch. He works at our ranch. Now that we have that little introduction out of the way, how about if you fork over the horse?"

Tony kicked at a chunk of snow with the toe of his boot. It was obvious he was trying to consider what to do.

"We're not going anywhere till you do," Lyssa added, crossing her arms in front of her chest.

"That's right," Mitch said.

"So we're just going to stand here in a stalemate," Tony muttered, his eyes darting back and forth between Mitch and Lyssa.

"Check," Lyssa replied easily.

"Your horses are going to get sore muscles standing there in this cold," Tony pointed out.

Mitch climbed off Cody. "Not if you let us see what you're hiding," he said, looking at Lyssa.

Blue pawed at the ground again, impatient to be off. "Sorry, big guy," Lyssa murmured, stroking him under his jaw, where he liked to be scratched. "We've got to stand our ground here till the bogeyman of the Beartooth Mountains stops playing chess and hands over the goods."

Tony leaned against a rock, crossing his arms in front of his chest and grinning so that Lyssa could see an even row of white teeth. "Seeing as how I'm not handing over anything, you'll be there for a while," he said to Blue. Then, looking over at Lyssa, he added, "You really ought to take that horse home and give him a nice warm bran mash."

"That would only warm him for about ten minutes," Lyssa shot back. "If you knew anything at all about horses, you'd know that. If Blue here ate plain old hay, he'd stoke his fire for at least four hours."

"I've never worried about having to keep horses

warm in weather like this before," the guy muttered, half to himself.

"Whatever. Anyway, who are you to tell me how to take care of anything?" Lyssa exclaimed.

At that, the guy took off his black cowboy hat and bowed. "I already told you who I was—at the dance, remember? Tony Ransom, at your service," he said with mock gallantry.

Startled, Lyssa regarded him. "Ransom. That's not your last name," she said curtly. "You just made that up. Are you trying to say that I have to pay ransom for the horse?"

Tony's low laughter floated around them, infuriating Lyssa beyond belief. "Ransom?" he asked, seeming to consider her words. "I hadn't thought of that, but it sounds like a good idea. What are you prepared to pay? Maybe you could trade me your horse for mine, sight unseen."

Lyssa was about to snap something back when she saw that he was joking. "Ha ha. Aren't you funny," she said sarcastically.

"Who knows?" Tony continued. "You might make a really good trade, even though your horse is pretty fit. Amazing what fitness gallops can do."

Lyssa nodded, surprised. "What do you know about fitness gallops?"

Tony ignored her. "And he looks incredibly athletic. Good slope to his shoulder. I'll bet he's a good mover. Probably really wows the judges in the dressage arena." He studied Blue closely, seeming to take in every detail.

So he knows something about horses after all, Lyssa thought fleetingly as she shivered. Standing still, she could really feel the cold.

"Are we going to stand around and talk horses all day?" Mitch said impatiently.

Lyssa shot him a look that said, *Be quiet and let me handle this.*

Mitch shrugged and flicked his reins against his hand.

Lyssa tucked her hands under her arms to warm them while she considered what to do next. She didn't like being toyed with by Tony any better than Mitch did, but something told her she'd better take things slowly.

Tony looks hungry! she suddenly thought.

Reaching over to Blue's saddlebag, Lyssa untied the leather thongs and pulled out some of the food she'd stashed earlier. Out of the corner of her eye, she saw she'd gotten Tony's attention.

"I sure am hungry from tracking you all these hours," she said with exaggerated loudness while she handed Mitch a granola bar. "Guess Mitch and I will just hang out right here and munch on these goodies while you continue your little game of stalemate."

"Suit yourself. I'm not going anywhere," Tony replied.

"Mmm. Raisins and chocolate chips," Lyssa said, unwrapping her granola bar. She took a huge bite, chewing slowly and deliberately, all the while looking at Tony's green eyes. "What's next? A homemade apple-cinnamon muffin, or should I wolf down some hot soup?"

He looks hungry, but he's not going to crack, Lyssa thought as she hatched a plan. Reaching back into her saddlebag, she pulled out a couple of carrots and fed them to Blue.

"Did you ever meet a horse that doesn't like carrots?" Lyssa mused, glancing over at Tony pointedly while Blue crunched.

"All right, all right," he exclaimed. "You didn't by any chance bring any extra hay or anything, did you? Give me some food for Lady Jane, and I'll fill you in."

Lyssa beamed. Her ploy had been successful.

Aloud she said, "But you'd better fill me in good," and handed over some feed and carrots. She threw in the Thermos of hot soup for good measure.

"I'll be right back," Tony growled, grabbing everything. "Don't try to follow me," he added darkly as he disappeared around the pile of rocks.

Lyssa smiled at Mitch. "Now we're getting somewhere," she whispered.

The ranch hand scowled. "Let's just bust through there and see what's going on," he hissed, leaning down to rub Cody's legs. "I'm way tired of this, and so is my horse."

Lyssa shook her head. "Be patient," she said, turning Blue in small circles to keep him moving.

Straining her ears, Lyssa could hear Tony's footsteps crunching through the snow for a few seconds, then the sound died away. Chewing her granola bar slowly, she wondered if maybe she ought to do what Mitch said. If she climbed back on Blue, she'd have the advantage over Tony, since he was on foot. She could get to the horse first. But on the other hand, Tony would tell her the real story only if he trusted her.

Blue stepped in front of her and snuffled her pockets intently, looking for another carrot.

"You're right, Blue," she said softly, stroking his nose thoughtfully. "We can bide our time."

A few moments later Tony reappeared. Sitting on the rock, he opened the Thermos and poured the soup.

The steam rose from the cup as he inhaled it appreciatively before sipping.

"So, whatever your name is, it's time to spill," Mitch muttered. "All of us are getting cold and tired of standing around."

"My name really is Tony Ransom," the guy said. "I didn't make it up, though I have to say, this 'ransom' isn't half bad."

Lyssa shrugged and continued circling Blue. After a few more circles Lyssa stopped Blue and started gently massaging him, starting at his withers and working her way back and down his legs.

"Homemade?" Tony asked, holding up the Thermos.

"Enough small talk. I kept my end of the deal," Lyssa snapped while her fingertips made their way over Blue. "Now, out with it. What are you doing up here in this wilderness, and why are you hiding a horse?"

Tony grinned. "What else would a respectable horse thief do?" he asked.

"Cool it with the jokes!" Lyssa snapped, stamping her numb foot and wincing at the pain as she did so.

Tony shook his head. "I'm not joking," he replied with total seriousness. "I am a horse thief, I guess. I've stolen a mare, and I've been trying to hide her. I figured no one would be idiot enough to ride out in this weather to try to find us."

"Who are you calling an idiot?" Mitch demanded, taking a step toward Tony.

Lyssa held Mitch back with a warning look. "Look, Tony, Mitch and I aren't idiots," she muttered angrily.

"I didn't mean idiot, exactly," Tony responded. "I meant I didn't think anyone would bother trying to track us. It's cold out here, and dangerous. People generally have better things to do—like stay inside where it's warm."

Lyssa continued massaging Blue. "Maybe some of us like it outside—though we do know better than to come up here during a snowstorm," she admitted. "But quite honestly, we don't like horse thieves very much."

Tony finished his soup, screwing the cap back on the Thermos. "As a general rule, I don't like them very much myself," he stated calmly.

Lyssa regarded the guy, the wheels turning in her head. She couldn't help feeling a great swelling of sadness. Though she had been annoyed at the way Tony teased her like a cat toying with a mouse, she couldn't help but be impressed by how knowledgeable he was about horses and how caring he was, making sure his horse had something to eat before he did. But unfortunately, no matter how nice a guy Tony seemed to be, if he'd stolen a horse, there was only one thing to do. She and Mitch had to summon the sheriff.

"Well, Tony," Lyssa said as she climbed back in Blue's saddle, "It's been real, tracking you up here and having lunch together. But I'm afraid my friend and I need to head back down and turn you in. You could make it easier on all of us and grab that horse and come with us, or you could stay here and wait for the authorities. It's up to you."

Tony stood up, searching Lyssa's face closely. "You can forget about me coming back with you," he said.

Lyssa shrugged. "Fine, play hardball if you want to," she said. "But don't kid yourself: You will be found."

With that, she wheeled Blue around, intending to set off down the trail.

"Wait," Tony called out. "Don't go yet. There's more to the story!"

"This had better be good!" Lyssa yelled as she spun Blue to face Tony.

"Stay here," Tony commanded, ducking behind the rocks.

Mitch raised an eyebrow. "This disappearing act is getting really old, Lyss," he mumbled.

When Tony emerged a few moments later, he was leading a gorgeous bay mare into the clearing.

Lyssa felt the color drain from her face.

It was Mystic!

9

"WHAT ARE *YOU* DOING WITH MYSTIC?" LYSSA AND MITCH gasped at the same time.

Lyssa's eyes swept over the well-built mare, who was now wearing her thick winter coat. Her ears pricked and she lifted her elegant head, nostrils flaring as she drank in the chill wind.

"I've named her Lady Jane," Tony countered.

Lyssa shook her head. "No, her name's Mystic," she said quietly. "She belongs—belonged—to a friend of mine. She's been lame—and you dragged her all the way up here? That's cruel!"

"She hasn't taken a lame step since I've known her!" Tony replied.

Lyssa still couldn't believe her eyes. "*This* is the horse you stole?"

Tony reached up to straighten her forelock. "Yep," he answered.

"Well, she looks good, at least," Lyssa said, studying Mystic intently. She didn't appear any worse for her adventures over the past few days.

Tony bristled. "Why wouldn't she look good?" he demanded. "I've taken excellent care of her."

"Yeah, right," Lyssa said with a snort. "You take her from her forever home where she was to be loved and cared for the rest of her life. You take her traipsing through the snow for miles, stable her in an equipment shed, drag her up into the mountains, and hide her behind a rock pile. Now that's what I call A-plus horse care!"

"You have no idea what you're talking about!" Tony flashed. "And anyway, *you're* the one letting your horse stand out here in the cold while you're lecturing me. You have the nerve to tell me I don't know how to take care of a horse?"

Lyssa looked guiltily over at Blue. "Well, you're right about the standing part," she said, starting to walk Blue in small circles again. "Let's get moving— down the mountain. You have to bring Mystic back home. Mrs. Peters must be going ballistic wondering where she is!"

Tony laughed bitterly. "You're right. Mrs. Peters probably *is* going ballistic. But not for the reason you think."

"What are you talking about?" Lyssa was mystified.

Tony sighed heavily and stroked Mystic's soft muzzle. "Mrs. Peters is not who you think she is. She's charming, and she can make anyone believe anything they want to believe, that's for sure," Tony spat out. "But she's also the biggest liar on either side of the Rockies. She's not providing a home for any poor creatures."

Lyssa frowned. "But I've heard she's sweet and loves animals," she said.

"I think I'm falling a little behind here," Mitch said in a bewildered voice.

Lyssa realized she hadn't told Mitch about Gabriela and how she had found Mystic a new home.

"Mrs. Peters rents the old Fowler place. I'll explain later," she said quickly to Mitch. Turning back to Tony, she said, "My friend told me she runs this really great retirement home for animals. Mrs. Peters has all kinds of rescues that she's taken in at the ranch. Gabriela went over and saw it for herself. It was clean and well kept, and she had horses, cattle, and—I don't know, a whole bunch of animals everywhere."

"It's a way station," Tony said flatly, watching as snowflakes started falling gently from the sky. "C'mon. The weather's turning bad again. Let's go under the overhang where I've been keeping Lady Jane, and I'll tell you what really goes on at that 'forever home' you've been jabbering about."

Lyssa and Mitch followed Tony around the rock pile to a large overhang that Lyssa recognized instantly. It was Roger's Ridge. Tony had created fluffy bedding for Mystic out of leaves. They ground-tied the horses. Mitch stayed near Blue and Mystic while Lyssa walked over to Tony.

"Well?" she demanded.

Tony sat on a boulder, but Lyssa remained standing.

"Mrs. Peters has the big ranch, all right," he said. "And she has lots of animals there. Seems all kinds of people buy into her story that she'll retire their animals. Thing is, she does keep them—for a while." Tony paused, then blurted out, "Then when she runs short of cash, she sells them to the meatpackers or anyone who offers her any amount of money!"

"No way!" Lyssa exploded. "She said she keeps them forever. In fact, she told Gabriela to come visit anytime!"

Tony smiled, but his eyes held no hint of merriment. "That's her line," he said. "She tells people to stop by the ranch. The thing is, they do for the first couple of weeks or so. Before you know it, they become too busy and involved in other things. The visits become less frequent. Then one day Mrs. Peters calls Lowell Brothers. They don't ask questions. They get a cheap source of meat, and that's that. If someone happens to visit, they're told their horse just happens to be out at an upper pasture."

Lyssa put her hand to her mouth. She felt sick. "That's horrible!" she exclaimed.

Tony kicked at a clump of dirty snow at his feet. "Uh-huh," he agreed. "And once most people drive all the way to the ranch for nothing, they usually don't come back. Instead they take the lazy way out and phone, and Mrs. Peters tells them what they want to hear."

Lyssa was so shocked that for a moment she couldn't speak. When she finally found her tongue, she looked steadily at Tony said, "So you stole Mystic to save her."

Tony nodded. "The minute I saw her, I knew she was special. I couldn't let anything happen to her. You see, I just moved here from Arizona because I'd been promised a great job with a training barn. But when I got here, the owner told me he'd decided to close down his operation. The only place I could get work was with

Mrs. Peters. She didn't think I would catch on to her scheme, I guess. But one afternoon when she thought I was gone, the meatpackers' truck came. It explained why animals kept disappearing. I didn't let on that I suspected anything, and tried to figure out what to do."

Lyssa gazed at Blue and then at Mystic. She could hardly believe what she was hearing. Of course, Tony could be lying to cover up something else. Why shouldn't she believe Tony was making all this up?

Narrowing her eyes as she studied Tony's face, she asked bluntly, "Do you swear you're telling me the truth?"

Tony nodded. "You have no idea how much I wish I weren't," he said.

"You could be saying all this so you have an excuse for stealing Mystic," Mitch muttered. "I mean, why couldn't you just call the sheriff's office and tell them everything?"

Tony stood up and sighed. "I got into trouble with the law once before in Arizona. I'd caught some men I worked for at a racing stable trying to mess with horses' identities in a betting scheme." Tony's eyes darkened as he continued. "They were pretty powerful. They turned the story around, and it ended up that I got accused—and they got away. It got cleared up, but the authorities told me I'd better keep my nose clean from now on. I figured no one knew me around these parts, so they wouldn't believe me. Mrs. Peters is a pretty good talker. I was sure she'd persuade everyone I was the bad guy."

Lyssa bit her lip as she watched the snow swirling gently around them. She glanced at Mitch, then turned back to Tony. "We have to nail this woman. Do you have proof?"

Tony walked over to a saddlebag he'd slung over a rotted log. "This, maybe?" he said, pulling out a bent license plate. "It fell off the meatpackers' truck a while ago. I kept it in case I needed it."

Lyssa glanced at the license plate, then handed it to Mitch.

"Well, I guess if the sheriff ran it through the computer and it was registered to a meatpacker, it would confirm your story," Mitch said.

Tony jammed his hands into the pockets of his jeans. "Well, then, let's go. To tell you the truth, I had no idea how to get back down the mountain after that avalanche. And honestly, I wasn't even sure where I was going in the first place. I had this half-baked idea of hiding out in some outbuildings around here till I figured out what to do with Lady Jane—I mean Mystic. But then I was forced up here to get away from you," Tony said, looking at Lyssa.

Mitch tightened Cody's cinch, ready to set off.

Lyssa gazed at Mystic before turning to ready Blue. "You know, Mystic's been lame. It's her left fore. No one could figure out why. That's why my friend had to retire her—which is how she ended up at Mrs. Peters's ranch in the first place."

"Hasn't been lame since I've been around her," Tony countered, furrowing his brow. Walking over to the mare, he ran his hand down her leg, then picked up her foot. Taking out a hoof pick, he gently worked the pick around the frog and touched the sole. With his fingers, he felt around the coronet band and the hoof wall. "Someone's really botched up her shoeing," he muttered.

"The vet couldn't find anything," Lyssa said defensively. Pausing, she added, "She was supposed to be an eventing horse."

Tony gently set down Mystic's foot. "An eventing horse, huh?" A grin spread across his face. "I want to be an eventer."

Lyssa looked at Tony in surprise. "You? I haven't met too many people around here who know about eventing."

"That was why I came to Montana in the first place," Tony explained. "My friend from school knew this eventer in Billings—Hank Kelleher. That was the person whose barn I was going to work at."

"I know Hank," Lyssa said. "He did pretty well on the eventing circuit, but I did hear he went out of business."

Tony nodded. "I guess I'll have to go back to Arizona," he muttered, saddling Mystic with a western saddle. He tossed his saddlebag over the cantle and set the bridle on the shoulder, leading her forward with her lead rope.

Mitch led Cody out from the overhang, shooting Lyssa an I-don't-believe-him look.

Lyssa furrowed her brow at Tony. "If you're telling the truth, why can't you just find another job around here?" she asked.

"The sheriff will never believe me," he stated. "You'll see."

"Well, then," Lyssa exclaimed, "I'm going to go see Mrs. Peters myself and confront her."

"Don't be a dork," Tony replied. "She'll fool you the way she fools everybody."

"I wouldn't be so sure about that," Lyssa snapped.

Taking Blue's reins, she led Blue out into the snow and mounted. She watched Tony climb aboard Mystic and noted how light and easy his seat was.

"We'll go to our place," Lyssa said, her mind racing as the three of them set off down the mountain. "Dad and Uncle Cal will be off checking on the cattle, so if you just hang out in the barn, they won't even know you're there. Mitch will make sure you don't bolt, and I'll drive out to the Fowler place and see for myself."

"I don't know about this, Lyss," Mitch exclaimed. "What will your folks say if they do stumble on us? They won't be thrilled if it turns out I'm hiding a horse thief. I think we'd just better call the sheriff's office and let them handle it."

"That comes later. But first I want to check out Mrs. Peters with my own eyes," Lyssa said, making her way carefully down the mountain.

"Well, your timing couldn't be better," Tony said bitterly. "I know she's expecting a visit from the meat-packers this afternoon. That's what prompted me to make my move with Mystic. I wanted her to be long gone when that truck pulled up."

"Then I'm going to be there," Lyssa exclaimed grimly. Her head was still spinning with all that she had heard.

By now the snow was falling more heavily, swirling gently around them. For a while no one spoke, but Lyssa could tell Tony was enthralled by what he was seeing. His eyes softened, and he wore a half smile.

I wonder what he's thinking, Lyssa thought, studying him discreetly from a distance.

"The way the snow is falling, it looks like feathers," Tony said when the trail widened enough for them to ride side by side.

Lyssa nodded, looking at Tony's handsome profile out of the corner of her eye. "You're right," she said softly. "Only trust me, it didn't seem like feathers yesterday when it formed an avalanche and nearly buried Blue and me."

"My first avalanche," Tony said. "Luckily, Lady—I mean Mystic and I were above it. We could see it barreling down the mountainside."

Lyssa glared at Tony. "See what you got me into?"

"You didn't have to follow me," Tony replied. But then he grinned and shook his head. "But I'm glad you did—I think."

Lyssa squeezed Blue's sides gently with her heels, moving ahead of Tony. She didn't want to think about what he'd just said. There was no way she wanted to have any more fuzzy feelings about the cute guy riding next to her—not until she knew for sure that he was telling the truth and that he hadn't stolen Mystic for real!

When they arrived at the ranch, Lyssa slid off Blue and handed his reins over to Mitch.

"Give me the keys to your truck," she said, her eyes darting around, looking for any signs of her parents. "I can't take Tin Annie—she's on her last legs. And if you see Mom and Dad or anyone, make up a story."

"Maybe we ought to all go," Mitch said, hesitating. "You could end up in real trouble out there."

"I don't think Mrs. Peters is dangerous, exactly," Tony said thoughtfully. "Just sneaky and money-hungry."

Lyssa shook her head and patted her pocket. "Don't worry. Even if she gets ornery, I've got Mrs. Lattimer's cell phone with me," she said. "I'll call if anything happens."

"You can't just show up unannounced," Tony added. "She might guess you're up to something."

Lyssa cocked her head. "I'll pretend I'm looking for a home for my dog."

Mitch reluctantly handed over his keys, and Lyssa watched as they led the horses around the back of the barn.

Glancing at the house, Lyssa jumped into the truck. Soon she was barreling down the road in the direction of the Fowler place. When she spotted the mailbox with *Peters* scrawled over the faded name of the former occupant, she turned the wheel and started down the long dirt road.

It had been years since Lyssa had been on the property. The last time had been when she had gone to a birthday party for Libby Fowler, who'd moved away shortly after that. The place hadn't changed much since then, Lyssa thought, looking around as she pulled up in front of the barn.

As she cut the motor, several dogs ran out, barking. Stepping out of the truck, Lyssa crouched down to pet them.

They seem a little thin, but not starved or anything, Lyssa thought.

As Lyssa straightened, her eyes swept the yard, and she studied the large, weathered barn surrounded by several small corrals with shelters in each of them. From where she stood, she could see that the corrals contained a few shaggy horses and some cattle standing out in the open air. Even though the corrugated roofs offered shelter from the elements, Lyssa saw that, like many horses and cattle, they preferred to stay outside in the snow, their tails to the wind. A few yards from the house, Lyssa could see a low building that she guessed was a kennel and another building that looked as though it housed chickens. A deafening cacophony of animal sounds filled the air.

All in all, it was a clean, decently kept place.

Lyssa's head snapped up as a figure in a yellow jacket emerged from the kennel and headed toward her.

I've seen that yellow jacket before, Lyssa thought, squinting as she tried to place it.

"Can I help you?" the woman asked as she approached.

It was the woman who had tried to take the puppy from her at the feed store!

10

"WE'VE MET, HAVEN'T WE?" THE WOMAN ASKED, PEERING closely at Lyssa.

Lyssa nodded. "Sort of. I—I was the one who adopted that Great Dane at the feed store," she said slowly.

"Oh, yes. The pedigreed one," Mrs. Peters replied, her voice suddenly cool.

"Seems I made a mistake taking him home, and I just can't keep him," Lyssa said. "He's just too—too big and rambunctious. I've heard you take in rescues."

Mrs. Peters smiled slowly. "That's right," she said, her voice suddenly becoming soft like a purr.

"Can you adopt another dog?" Lyssa asked.

The woman started to nod eagerly, then seemed to

check herself. "Of course, I'm kind of full right now."

Lyssa pretended to sigh. "You've got lots of dogs?" she asked.

"Lots of everything," the woman said. "Horses, cattle, even a llama someone decided he didn't want anymore. Can you believe how people shed animals just like they cast off old clothes?"

"Do people really dump horses?" Lyssa asked, faking innocence.

The woman nodded. "Pedigreed ones, too, the ones that are worth some bucks," she said. "Just the other day, some girl handed me a real looker. Said she was a fancy show horse, only she was lame. Didn't look lame to me. But I took her."

"A show horse?" Lyssa exclaimed, hoping the lady didn't hear the excitement in her voice. "Can I see her?"

Mrs. Peters let out a sigh. "She's out in the upper pasture. I'd have my new hired hand take you to her, only I don't know where he is at the moment." Half to herself, she added, "I don't know why I waste good money on that good-for-nothing boy."

Lyssa looked around, pretending not to pay attention to the woman's reference to Tony. "You keep these animals forever, huh?" she asked casually.

The woman nodded. "That's right. I feed them and care for them and let them live out their days. Costs a lot to feed them and all, but what's money?"

As Mrs. Peters said the word *money*, it seemed to Lyssa that her eyes narrowed slightly. Lyssa felt a chill travel up her spine.

Mrs. Peters started toward the barn. "There are even more inside the barn. Come see for yourself," she said, throwing open the door.

Inside, Lyssa saw several cats nestled in the hay. There were a couple of sheep and two heifers. In the corner, Lyssa saw several miniature goats in a small pen.

"See? I have my own peaceable kingdom here," Mrs. Peters said. "Now, about that pup. You'll bring his papers, right?"

Lyssa nodded. "Sure thing. They won't be of any use to me."

"So when will you be bringing the dog by?" the woman asked in what seemed to Lyssa to be an overly casual tone.

"Oh, this afternoon. Right away," Lyssa said, walking toward the barn door. "But first I'd kind of like to look around some more."

Mrs. Peters seemed annoyed. "Nothing much more

for you to see," she said briskly, following Lyssa closely. "The place is kept up. The animals are well fed."

It seemed to Lyssa that the woman was awfully impatient. She glanced at her watch pointedly and frowned.

"Well, I can see you really take care of everything around here," Lyssa said, stalling now, wondering how long she could wait for the Lowell Brothers truck Tony had said would come.

Just then she heard the low rumble of a truck turning onto the dirt road. Mrs. Peters set her lips in a straight line. "Who can that be?" she asked, nervously glancing at Lyssa. "Oh, it's Lowell Brothers, the irrigation pipe layers. So why don't you run off now and go bring me that pup."

"Will do," Lyssa said calmly, studying the truck as it came closer.

Good one, Mrs. Peters, Lyssa thought. *Try Lowell Brothers, the meatpackers!*

"But first, if you don't mind, I think I'll go say hello to the horses in the corrals," Lyssa called casually, though her stomach churned as she realized just why the Lowell Brothers were there.

They're about to make another animal pickup! she reminded herself, horrified. *One of these horses is doomed!*

"You can say hello to the horses when you bring that puppy back," Mrs. Peters said, obviously struggling to keep her tone even.

Lyssa noticed a muscle twitching in Mrs. Peters's face. Finally the woman turned toward the Lowell Brothers truck and held up her hand for the driver to stop.

"Now what do I do?" Lyssa mumbled to herself, heart pounding, while she darted over to the corral. Several horses came over to investigate her, to see if she'd brought them any treats. She searched her pockets while her mind raced.

What can I do about Mrs. Peters selling animals to the meatpackers? she thought miserably. *She's not abusing them. Even if I find it disgusting, legally it's her business.*

Absently she continued searching her pockets till she found and pulled out a carrot, which she broke into pieces. Moving down the line, she fed each horse, wondering just which one the truck was here to haul off. As a chestnut gelding nibbled at the piece of carrot, she stroked his forelock and ran her finger over his distinctive snip. Snips, Lyssa knew, were as individual as fingerprints, and no two horses had snips exactly the same.

"Hey, guy," she murmured. "I wish you could talk

and tell me what's going on here." Suddenly Lyssa froze.

That snip! She'd seen a diagram of it on a stolen-horse bulletin posted over at Beartooth Feed and Seed. The way the patch of white trailed down the pictured horse's nose was so striking, it had really stood out at the time. Lyssa gasped. There was no doubt about it—she was looking at a stolen horse!

Lyssa's thoughts raced. If she called the authorities, they could come to the ranch and nail Mrs. Peters for being in possession of stolen property. Reaching for Mrs. Lattimer's cell phone, Lyssa pressed the power button, poised to punch in the number for the sheriff. The office wasn't too far down the highway.

"No!" Lyssa groaned when she saw the words No Service light up on the phone's tiny screen.

She resisted the urge to drop the useless device and grind it into the ground with the heel of her boot. Now she'd have to take off in Mitch's truck and hightail it to the sheriff's office. Of course, the minute she left, the Lowell Brothers truck could haul one of the horses off, and it would be too late. No evidence, no case! Mrs. Peters could continue to run her sneaky operation and no one would be the wiser.

Lyssa bit her lip as she looked over at the woman, who was now talking with the driver.

She's probably telling him to wait till I'm outta here before he starts loading up animals, Lyssa thought. *Well, if I can't get the sheriff out here in time to see this guy, I'll just have to bring him to the sheriff!*

A plan was beginning to take shape in Lyssa's brain. Thinking fast, she remembered an old western bridle she'd seen on the floor of Mitch's truck. One of the guests had broken a rein over the holidays, and Mitch had evidently forgotten to take it to the tack repair shop last time he'd gone into town. Walking quickly to the truck, Lyssa opened the door and grabbed it. Quickly she tied the broken rein in a knot before shoving it under her parka, her hand wrapped around the cold metal of the bit to try to warm it up as much as she could before she pressed it into service.

"Just getting some treats for the horses," Lyssa sang out as she caught Mrs. Peters staring at her with narrowed eyes while the truck driver took a puff of his cigarette.

"Don't feed my animals!" Mrs. Peters snapped.

Rushing back over to the corral, Lyssa's heart started pounding.

This is about the craziest thing I've ever done, she thought, slipping through the fence and running up to the horse. *A million things could go wrong.*

"Hey, sweetie," she said, stopping to hold out her hand. The chestnut snorted suspiciously and stepped back. "I'm sorry. I know this is rather sudden. I have no idea who you are or what you're doing here, but I promise you, it's for your own good."

With a quick motion, Lyssa slipped the warmed bit in the horse's mouth and pulled the split-eared bridle over his ears, crooning to him the whole time. Then, grabbing a hunk of mane, she jumped and swung a leg neatly over his back.

The next second, the chestnut lunged forward, and Lyssa made a stab for the reins, neck-reining the horse in the direction of the gate.

"You there! What are you doing?" the woman yelled angrily.

Lyssa quickly leaned over, flicking the latch and opening the gate. Then she nudged the chestnut's sides and shot out of the corral, leaving the gate open behind her.

The chestnut scooted sideways, nearly dumping Lyssa in the snow, but somehow she managed to hang on.

"I know, this is totally unfair, Snip. But you're Exhibit A, and I just don't have any choice!" Lyssa exclaimed, using every riding technique she knew to bring the surprised horse back under her.

"Get off that horse this minute!" Mrs. Peters shouted menacingly.

"I think not!" Lyssa yelled.

With that, she sat back on her seat bones and made a kissing noise. Digging her heels into Snip's sides, she tore past the astonished woman and the truck driver and down the dirt road leading to the highway.

As Lyssa galloped toward the highway, she heard the sound of a car engine starting up behind her. Looking over her shoulder, she saw that it was Mrs. Peters—driving Mitch's truck! She'd left the keys in the ignition.

How absolutely brainless was that? Lyssa scolded herself, rocking forward and leaning against the chestnut's neck, sending him forward for all he was worth. *That horrible woman is going to run you down in your best friend's truck!*

The chestnut stretched low as he sprinted across the parking area, but he was no Thoroughbred, and he had trouble sustaining his pace. Lyssa charged up the dirt road leading toward the mailbox, trying to decide what to do. Within seconds the truck was tailing her.

Lyssa looked desperately around her. It seemed obvious to head up to the highway, but then what? Once she got up to the road, she'd be trapped by the fence line running down both sides for miles. If she tried to cut in, she'd be running on slick, icy asphalt, probably smack dab in front of a huge semi.

"Road pizza," Lyssa muttered, her forehead breaking out in a sweat in spite of the near-freezing temperature.

It was then that she spotted a break in the fence just up ahead. Slowing the chestnut momentarily, Lyssa applied a neck rein again, turning the horse sharply and steering him through the narrow opening. He responded instantly.

Must be a cutting horse, she thought fleetingly, her feet scraping against the fence posts. For one terrifying instant she thought she was going to be scraped off.

Ha! Lyssa thought with satisfaction as Snip galloped on. Looking over her shoulder, she could see the truck stop at the fence and Mrs. Peters's face grimacing horribly at her as she bolted across the snowy expanse.

"You won't get away with this!" shouted the woman, her voice echoing.

"Neither will you," Lyssa growled, turning back to the chestnut and allowing her arms and shoulders to move in rhythm with the action of his choppy stride.

Twenty minutes later she slowed the horse and brought him to a halt in the paved parking lot of the tiny sheriff's office.

A uniformed deputy who was just getting out of her patrol car glanced at Lyssa as she slid off, automatically reaching over to feel the chestnut's chest.

"Is everything okay, young lady?" the deputy asked.

Struggling to catch her breath, Lyssa nodded. "Yes, ma'am. I mean no. I mean, I'd like to report a crime."

11

AN HOUR LATER THE DEPUTY DROPPED LYSSA OFF AT THE wooden sign at the entrance to Black Thunder Ranch.

"We'll be sending out some officers right away to question Tony," the deputy said before taking off down the road.

Lyssa walked slowly toward the ranch house, her head spinning from all that had happened. As she got closer to the house, she could see that her mom and Uncle Cal had spotted her. The puppy was running around them in circles, stopping every so often to bite at the snow. Drawing closer, Lyssa saw that her mom's expression was stern.

Yikes. I'm in for it now, Lyssa thought.

"Lyssa!" Mrs. Hynde rapped out. "Where have you been? I thought I told you not to leave the ranch!"

Lyssa shook her head and stopped in front of her mother. "No, you didn't—not exactly," she said truthfully, digging the heel of her boot into the snow.

Mrs. Hynde placed her hands on her hips. "You have some explaining to do, young lady."

"Your dad's in the barn with Mitch and some stranger who won't give his name, trying to figure out why Mystic is here instead of at the Lattimers' place," Uncle Cal said. "Those boys aren't talking much, but they seem to be plenty jumpy about you."

Lyssa reached for the puppy and snorted. "Well, they can stop worrying about me," she replied. "I've already been talking to the sheriff."

"The sheriff?" her mom echoed.

Lyssa turned as Tony and Mitch came trudging up from the barn, followed by her dad.

"Well?" Mitch demanded. His face was drawn and tight, and Lyssa could see the muscles working in her jaw.

"I think we've got ourselves a horse thief," she said quietly.

Tony stopped as all eyes turned to him.

"Well, this is a first," drawled Uncle Cal, glaring at

Tony. "We've never had one of those here at Black Thunder Ranch before. So why are you helping out a horse thief, Mitch?"

"Ask her," Mitch replied, jerking a thumb at Lyssa. "She's the one who got me into this mess."

"This is Tony Ransom," Lyssa jumped in quickly. "And at this point I'm not sure if *he's* exactly a horse thief."

"Ma'ams. Sirs," Tony said, taking off his black hat and nodding politely.

Her dad opened his mouth and closed it. Uncle Cal removed his battered cowboy hat and scratched his head. "Lyssa, haven't you given this old man enough gray hair?" he asked.

As the wind began to howl around them, the puppy whined.

Mrs. Hynde sighed and picked him up. "While you all sort this out, I'm taking this pup inside," she said. "He's shivering, and I'm freezing."

"It *is* cold out here," Lyssa's dad said, scowling. "Let's all go back to the barn and get to the bottom of this."

Where do I begin? Lyssa thought. She let out a deep sigh as she turned toward the barn.

Once inside the snug interior, Mr. Hynde motioned toward some hay bales that were lined up along the wall. "All right. Get comfortable. No one's going anywhere till I'm clear on exactly what's going on around here," he said, leaning against the tractor and nodding at Lyssa. "You first."

Mitch sat down, his long blue-jeaned legs stretched out in front of him, but Tony and Lyssa remained standing. Walking over next to the stall where Mystic was now housed, Lyssa recounted the events of the past few days, starting with the mysterious hoofprints and leading up to seeing the meatpackers' truck pulling up to the old Fowler place.

"And just when I started wondering what I could do even if I *could* prove Mrs. Peters was sending those animals to their death for money, I discovered a stolen horse on her property," Lyssa said. She looked at Tony sadly, an unspoken question in her eyes: *Did you know about this, too?*

Tony's head rose. "I knew about the other stuff, but I didn't know she had any stolen animals. I thought she got them all the way she got Mystic—freebies from people who didn't want to take care of their responsibilities anymore!"

"How do we know you're telling the truth?" Mitch burst out.

Lyssa searched Tony's green eyes. She saw no trace of dishonesty.

145

He's telling the truth, she thought.

Just then a siren split the air. Lyssa rushed over to the door and saw the red light on top of the sheriff's SUV that was approaching the barn.

She turned back quickly toward Tony and swallowed hard, unable to speak.

What if she was just seeing what she wanted to see in those eyes?

Two men came into the barn, one talking into a crackling radio.

"We're looking to question one Anthony Ransom," said one of the uniformed men, a burly, gray-haired man who seemed to be in charge.

"There's an office in the back where you can take him," Mr. Hynde said.

Lyssa looked at the ground as the two officers led Tony in the direction her father had pointed.

Just then Uncle Cal stepped in the door. "Come on, Lyssa, Mitch, Rob. Gwen and Marcy sent me down to fetch you all for supper."

Lyssa knew that he had been listening outside and waiting for the right moment to whisk them all away. Scowling as she strained to hear what was being said in the office, she debated telling Uncle Cal she'd come up later. But one look at her dad told her she'd better not even suggest such a thing.

Jamming her frozen hand into her parka pocket, Lyssa fingered the can of nonstick spray she still had in there as she followed her uncle and Mitch toward the house. If only she could hear exactly what Tony was saying!

As they neared the house Lyssa glanced over her shoulder in time to see Tony being led toward the sheriff's SUV. At the same time Tony looked over at her. He waved at Lyssa with a sad smile, and she gave him a fixed stare in return.

Are they taking him away because they think he's guilty? Lyssa wondered. *Is he going to go to jail?*

"We're off to pay a little visit to Mrs. Peters," one of the men called out to Lyssa's dad.

Tony's eyes met Lyssa's briefly. "Take care of Lady Jane," he said, tipping his hat and climbing into the car.

Lyssa nodded. "You mean Mystic," she called back, wondering what Tony was thinking. It would be horrible for him to have to face Mrs. Peters and accuse her to her face. Mrs. Peters would be furious when she found out that Tony had stolen Mystic. Gulping, Lyssa pictured the mare. While it was true that Mystic was out of danger now, she couldn't help wondering what would happen to her next. She'd have to call Gabriela and tell her everything.

Problem is, Gabriela's poor judgment put Mystic in

harm's way in the first place, Lyssa thought. Shaking her head, she decided she'd better find out more and consider everything before she called Gabriela. Glancing at her dad, she decided she just had to go and see Mystic for a moment.

"Give me two minutes. I'll be right up for supper, I promise," Lyssa called out as she turned and shot back into the barn. She went over to Mystic's stall and stepped inside, stroking the mare's nose. Mystic lifted her delicate head and nosed Lyssa, nibbling on her hair.

"You're such a sweetie," Lyssa murmured. "None of this ever should have happened to you. You deserve a good home and someone to really love you. If only I could keep you."

Knowing she'd better not dawdle any longer, Lyssa gave the mare one last pat, closed the stall door, and made her way up to the house. Stepping inside the kitchen, she sat at the table with her family, thinking about Mystic's soulful eyes. She ate mechanically, not tasting anything she was putting in her mouth. She half listened as her dad filled her mom and Aunt Gwen in, and she merely nodded whenever he looked at her to corroborate what he was saying.

"Once we know what's going on, I'll take you to get your truck," Uncle Cal said to Mitch after supper.

"Thanks," Mitch replied, standing up and placing

his napkin on the table. He looked at Lyssa. "Well, Lyss, this is the last time I lend you my truck. Can't have you leaving it all around town because you find a better mode of transportation," he joked.

Lyssa felt her cheeks heat up. "I'm sorry, Mitch," she said, feeling rotten. "I hope our villain didn't trash it, but if she did, I'll pay for the damage."

After helping with the dishes, Lyssa went over to the great room and grabbed a heavy blanket from the sofa. Wrapping herself up, she sat staring into the fire. She wouldn't be able to think straight till she knew what was going on with Tony. Only when she knew how it all came out was she going to call Gabriela.

Two hours later the phone rang, and Mr. Hynde grabbed it.

Lyssa studied his face as he listened. "I see," he said, his face creasing in a smile. "That's good news! Okay with us."

He hung up the phone and walked over to Lyssa.

"Well?" Lyssa asked impatiently.

"They've arrested Mrs. Peters for possession of stolen livestock," her dad said. "They called the owner of the stolen chestnut, and he's thrilled. And Tony's free to go. The officer at the desk said Tony will be along later to see Mystic one last time."

Lyssa felt relief flooding her. Tony wasn't a horse

thief! And she was going to see him again! She tried not to think about it being for the last time. It was funny, she thought. She'd only met him a couple of days ago, and already he was going to leave a hole in her life when he left.

Is that stupid or what? You need to get your brain unscrambled, she scolded herself, reaching for the phone to punch in the Lattimers' number.

"Gabriela, you're never going to guess where Mystic is," Lyssa burst out when her friend answered the phone.

"She's at Mrs. Peters's ranch, where she belongs," Gabriela sputtered. "Why wouldn't she be?"

"It's a long story," Lyssa explained. "Got a few minutes?"

Looking out the window at the snow-capped mountains while she retold the events of the past few days, Lyssa found herself having to stop frequently while Gabriela gasped, "No way!" Finally Lyssa finished.

"I just don't believe it!" Gabriela said explosively.

Lyssa toyed with the phone cord. "It's true. Every word," she said. "You'll probably read about it in tomorrow's newspaper."

"Jeez," Gabriela said.

"Aren't you excited? You can have Mystic back," Lyssa said, wondering why Gabriela didn't seem more horrified that she'd unwittingly almost sent Mystic to her death. She felt a surge of anger toward her friend.

Gabriela gulped audibly. "You know, Lyssa," she said after a long pause, "nothing's changed. Mystic is still going to be lame every time I turn around. I can't keep her. I just can't deal with a horse and a boyfriend and school and everything. I'll come over later to get her, but then I've got to figure out what to do next."

"Fine," Lyssa said, bristling. "But you ought to know that she's not lame now."

After she hung up the phone, she thought about what she had just heard. There was no getting around it: Gabriela had changed over the past few weeks. Horses were no longer important to her the way they once had been. Instead boys had taken over her brain.

Fine—I'm in no position to judge anyone. But I've got to think of a way to keep Mystic, Lyssa thought frantically.

As she turned this thought over in her mind, Lyssa scrunched down in the sofa and drummed her fingers on the armrest. There had to be some way to give Mystic a home, she thought fiercely. But then she sighed. She had to face it—she didn't have the money or the time for another horse right now. Even if she was able to get some sponsorship money, it would take everything she had to get Blue ready for the Olympics. There just wasn't energy to spare.

Maybe Tony can adopt Mystic! The thought made Lyssa sit upright so quickly that Duke, who had been sound asleep on the rug in front of the fire, woke and ambled over to her.

Tony obviously cares about her, Lyssa mused, stroking the sleepy puppy's head. He'd risked going to jail for her. When it came right down to it, he had risked his life as well.

But then Lyssa shook her head. It was no good concocting a fairy-tale ending in her head. One look at Tony told the story. He was a broke cowboy from Arizona who was in no position to pay to keep a horse that was prone to lameness. Mystic would have to go back to Gabriela's ranch, and Gabriela would waste no time finding another home for her.

Is Mystic going to end up in the back of the meatpackers' truck after all?

The thought horrified Lyssa, and she looked miserably out the picture window, seeing only a leaden sky and grim possibilities.

By the time Lyssa went down to the feed barn to start evening feeds, she was so depressed, she couldn't think straight. She toyed with the idea of begging her parents to figure out a way to keep Mystic, but even as she thought about it, she felt guilty. Mitch and her dad and uncle had enough work to do as it was. They didn't need a horse that would require veterinary care when there were so many other horses and cattle on the property needing attention.

"Why such a long face?" asked Mitch as he came up beside her. He grabbed armfuls of hay to throw onto the back of the hay truck. "Your good-looking guy friend is innocent."

"He's not my 'good-looking guy friend,'" she snapped.

Mitch flicked her long braid playfully. "C'mon," he said. "You teased me about Kelly, so I get to tease you about Tony."

"It's not the same," Lyssa muttered.

Mitch set down the hay and stood facing her. "Look," he said, "Mystic is safe, my truck wasn't damaged, and your folks are relieved everything turned out okay. All's well that ends well."

Letting out a sigh, Lyssa regarded her almost-brother and sighed. "It's not over yet," she said. "Gabriela doesn't want Mystic back. I think she's much more interested in some guy named Brendan than she is in what happens to that mare. I can't believe I was the one who helped her get Mystic in the first place. I thought she'd be a great owner."

Mitch slipped an arm around her shoulder. "Not everyone's as dedicated as you are, Lyssa," he said softly. "For some people, horses are just a phase, I guess."

Lyssa was embarrassed to see fat tears start to drip off her nose. She wiped them away quickly. "I can't let anything happen to Mystic."

Just then Lyssa heard a car pull up in front of the ranch house. She ran over to the door and looked out to see a shiny green truck park next to Tin Annie. Her heart pounded as she saw Tony climb out.

Nice truck, Lyssa thought in passing as she turned to start mixing up buckets of feed. But she kept glancing up, hoping Tony would come over to the feed barn to see her.

"Look, I'll do the feeds. You go see Tony," Mitch said.

I'm going to owe Mitch so many favors, I'll never get caught up, Lyssa thought with dismay. But she nodded gratefully. "Thanks, Mitch," she said, starting up the path to the parking area.

Moments later Lyssa and Tony were seated in the

great room, sipping hot chocolate. Duke kept jumping up on them, practically knocking their cups out of their hands. Although Lyssa tried to be stern with the puppy and make him behave, secretly she was glad that he was causing a commotion. It broke the tension and kept conversation light for a few moments.

Finally she took a deep breath and plunged in. "So the sheriff decided you were telling a straight story after all," she said, looking at Tony.

Tony nodded. "Actually, he decided I was innocent more quickly than you did," he said, grinning.

Lyssa looked at the floor, feeling her cheeks heat up. She had to admit she'd jumped to conclusions awfully quickly. Still, under the circumstances, how could she not have done so?

"Was it awful at Mrs. Peters's ranch?" she asked.

Tony scratched his jaw thoughtfully. "Yeah. She denied everything, of course. But soon she was confessing left and right and saying how she needed money. They cuffed her and hauled her off."

"What about the other animals on her place?" Lyssa asked.

"There's an old retired foreman and his wife who live on the place who take care of the animals," Tony said. "They had no idea what was going on. Mrs.

Peters was pretty sneaky about everything. I was hired because they were getting old and were having trouble keeping up. But they'll just have to pick up the slack again till the court figures out what to do. Anyway, unfortunately, there's not much stock left there."

Lyssa's stomach turned at the thought of the animals Tony hadn't been able to save—the ones who'd been sold before he'd gotten there.

"Where did you get this dog?" Tony asked, rubbing the puppy's ears.

"I adopted him," she said. "Someone left him at the Beartooth Feed and Seed. Can you believe it? Who'd leave such a cutie? I almost didn't take him, but you'll never believe who turned up and wanted to adopt him."

"Mrs. Peters," Tony guessed.

Lyssa nodded. "Of course, at the time I had no idea who she was, but I had the feeling she was more interested in his papers and what he might be worth than anything else," she explained.

"Wow," was all Tony said when she told him the rest of the story of how she'd ended up taking home Duke.

They sipped their hot chocolate quietly until Lyssa broke the silence. "Whose truck are you driving?" she asked bluntly.

"Mine," was Tony's reply. "And don't look so surprised. I didn't steal it."

Lyssa could feel her cheeks burning again. "I—I never said you stole it," she stammered.

Tony grinned, his green eyes lighting up. "No, but I could tell that's what you were thinking," he said.

"So now you can read my mind?" Lyssa shot back, embarrassed.

"Hate to tell you," Tony said, "but those eyes of yours give you away every time."

Lyssa glared as Tony went on. "Actually, I got my truck legitimately. I won it last February in California."

"Won it?" Lyssa asked. "What? Like on a TV game show or something?"

Tony shook his head. "I won the Grand Prix at Indio. It was a really big deal that was being sponsored by a car company. The truck was my prize."

"You ride jumpers?" Lyssa asked, looking at Tony with new eyes. In his faded jeans and worn western boots, he looked like anything but a Grand Prix show jumper. She had a hard time picturing him in tall black boots and a hunt coat.

"Not normally," Tony said. "I just did it because some friends of the family asked me to show one of their horses. His name was Panache, and he was so talented I couldn't say no. I told you, I'm an eventer. At least I want to be. I've got a ways to go."

Lyssa sat up. "I'm an eventer, too," she said. "And I've got a ways to go myself."

Like the Olympics, she added to herself.

Tony nodded. "I know all about you," he said. "I couldn't go anywhere around this town without hearing all about you and your fabulous horse and how you won some big four-star event in Kentucky last November."

Lyssa ground her toe into the braided rug at her feet, feeling a mixture of pride and embarrassment. "Well, I'm actually glad you're hearing about Blue and me," she confessed. "I'm about to hit every business in town to try to get some sponsorships. I need to stay afloat financially long enough to get to the Olympics. I'm hoping I can rustle up enough money to help with feed and maybe a trailer so I can get back east again for Rolex. My uncle Cal's rig won't make another trip to Kentucky, that's for sure. "

Tony sipped his hot chocolate. "You need a trailer? I know the owners of Huffman Trailers," he said. "Maybe I can tell them you're looking for a sponsor."

Lyssa's eyes widened in surprise. "I thought you were new around here," she said.

Tony nodded. "Kind of," he replied. "Just moved

here. But I've got family spread all over Billings. My cousins are named Huffman."

Lyssa grinned, shaking her head. Then she thought of something. "So why did you get a job with Mrs. Peters instead of just staying with relatives?"

Tony shrugged. "Pride, I guess," he said. "I'd finished my first year at Stanford, but I decided to quit. I missed riding. I can tell you, my parents didn't like it one bit. They want me to go to med school."

"You? Med school?" Lyssa raised her eyebrows.

"Don't look so shocked," Tony said. "I want to be a doctor one day—but not now. Right now I really just want to be around horses. After I quit school, I worked for a trainer in Arizona, but my parents kept pressuring me to return to school. So I decided to get away from home for a while. I got the job with Hank, but after that fell apart, I had to find work. The last thing I needed was for my parents to find out that I was mooching off the relatives. That's why I answered Mrs. Peters's ad."

"Arizona, California, Montana—you're all over the place," Lyssa exclaimed with wonder.

"All over the place is right. That's what my parents say," Tony said, nodding. "They say, 'Tony, you're almost nineteen. It's time to quit playing around and study so you can get into medical school.' I can't help it. I just want to learn to event and see a few places before I settle down at school, I guess."

Draining her hot chocolate, Lyssa got up and walked into the kitchen to rinse off her cup. "I know the feeling," she called. "I'm not even thinking about college right now. I can't wait to get back east again. And then I want to ride internationally and see the world."

Tony smiled as he came up next to her. "Sounds good to me," he said, holding his cup under the warm water.

Looking sideways at Tony, Lyssa could see that he was looking wistfully at the barn. "Gabriela is coming to get Mystic in a while," she said quietly.

"I'd better go say good-bye before I take off," Tony replied, his jaw tightening. "I guess it's back to Arizona for me, with my tail tucked between my legs. I don't think Montana and I get along after all."

Lyssa walked him to the door and watched him make his way to the barn. Then she turned and went into her room, closing the door behind her. Throwing herself prone on her bed, she stared moodily at the Navajo rug on her wood floor.

You've got to put all this behind you, she told herself sternly. *You don't have time to think about anything but Blue and wearing a USET team jacket.*

Though it all made perfect sense in her head, Lyssa

couldn't help feeling more depressed than she could ever remember. When she heard Gabriela's dad's rig come down the dirt road toward the house, she didn't even get up. There was no way she wanted to watch Tony look longingly at the horse he'd risked everything for while he turned over the lead rope to a stranger. She didn't want to see Gabriela reunite with her mare, knowing that she'd simply turn around and dump the mare somewhere else.

And admit it, Lyssa Hynde, she thought glumly. *What you really can't stand is the thought of seeing the taillights of Tony's truck disappear down the road.*

12

"GOOD MORNING, SLEEPYHEAD!"

Lyssa awoke with a start the next morning as her mom poked her head in the doorway. "This is the first time in a long time I've had to roust you out of bed," Mrs. Hynde said. "Are you feeling okay?"

Lyssa sat up, blinking, and pushed her covers down to the end of her bed. It was already eight in the morning.

I've never slept this late, Lyssa thought as the cobwebs slowly cleared and the events of the last few days rushed into her mind.

The sun was up, and the sky was blue and clear. From her bedroom window, Lyssa could see the snow sparkling like diamonds in the sunlight. But she felt a heaviness settle on her chest, and she scrunched down under her covers again, wishing she could just close her eyes and forget about everything that had happened.

Her mom furrowed her brow at her. "It isn't like you to sleep in so long," she said, walking over to lay a hand on her forehead.

"I'm okay," Lyssa replied, forcing a smile. "See? I'm getting up."

"All right," Mrs. Hynde said, starting down the hall. "But before you go anywhere this morning, we need to talk."

"About what?" Lyssa asked, but her mom was already gone.

Fine, Lyssa thought grumpily. *She's probably going to tell me I can't set foot off the ranch. Whatever. It's not like I want to go anywhere, anyway.*

After she showered and changed into warm clothes, she began brushing her hair, trying not to think about Mystic—or Tony.

But it was no use.

"Better get over it," Lyssa muttered, staring at her reflection. "They're gone and that's that. There's no time to mope about stuff you can't do anything about. You have to just get in gear and get on with everything."

While she finished getting ready, she considered her day. There were chores to do first, of course. Then she'd saddle up Blue. She'd take it easy since he'd been worked pretty hard over the last few days.

Maybe I'll head to the dressage arena and do a few suppling exercises, Lyssa thought, wrapping a leather tie around the end of her braid. *They won't be hard on Blue's poor feet and legs, and they'll do him some good.*

Lyssa walked into the kitchen, pasting on a smile as she greeted her mom and aunt. They were seated in front of a laptop at the kitchen table.

"We're trying to design our new brochure for the ranch," explained Mrs. Hynde. "What do you think so far?"

"Nice graphics," Lyssa said, peering at the screen before walking over to the coffeemaker.

"After we finish this, I'm heading into town. Do you need anything?" Aunt Gwen said gently.

Lyssa shook her head. "No, thanks. I'm off—I'm going to school Blue in the dressage arena," she replied, pouring a cup of coffee and grabbing a bran muffin. Opening the refrigerator door, she fished out some carrots.

"About that talk, Lyssa," her mom called as Lyssa darted from the warmth of the kitchen out into the cold morning air.

"We'll talk later, I promise," Lyssa called back, shivering as she hurried down the path leading away from the house. The last thing she needed right then was a lecture. She was already depressed enough without being told she was grounded on top of everything.

Gabriela is right. Parents can be so annoying sometimes, she fumed. The next instant she felt a wave of guilt. After all, she had betrayed their trust by going off to the mountains when she knew that it was strictly forbidden. Still, if she hadn't, there was no telling what might have happened. Tony might have made his way down just fine, and he might have been able to hide Mystic at some relative's place.

But then what? Tony couldn't have hidden forever. And who was to say they would have gotten down the mountain safely? Tony hadn't grown up around here. He didn't know the mountains the way Lyssa did. Most likely he and Mystic would have gotten trapped by snow and ice and ended up frozen or starved.

No, Lyssa thought, exhaling deeply, she was glad she had followed them. No matter how it had turned out.

Down at the barn, Lyssa inhaled the perfume of hay and horse, trying to draw comfort from the sweet, familiar smell. Picking up her grooming box, she walked wide past Mystic's stall, not wanting to look in and see it standing empty. She walked quickly over to Blue, who was whinnying like crazy, and slid open his door.

"Hey, sweetie, did you sleep as well as I did?" she murmured, holding out a carrot.

Blue grabbed the carrot greedily, and Lyssa stroked his neck just where his heavy winter blanket left off.

"We're going to go out there and practice and forget about everything but the Olympics," she said softly. "That okay with you? I'll bring my boom box, and maybe we'll do a few exercises to music."

Blue blew out his breath, sending carrot bits everywhere, and Lyssa laughed, feeling her spirits lift just a little.

"Well, look who decided to get out of bed and help out with the work around here," teased Mitch, stepping into the barn carrying a toolbox.

"Yeah, I believe you should try to help the little people when you can," Lyssa joked airily, brushing Blue's thick coat.

"Guess now that you're getting a big hunk of reward money, you've decided to become a princess, huh?" Mitch added.

Lyssa looked at him. "What are you talking about?"

"Reward money. Mr. Cooper's real glad you got his

horse back. He'd been offering a big reward. Guess it's yours."

Lyssa stopped brushing as she considered Mitch's words. Then she smiled. "Well, I'm just glad the horse is safe."

Suddenly a thought occurred to her. She could use the reward money to help pay for Mystic's upkeep. But as quickly as the idea came into her head, she dismissed it. Even if she had the money to maintain Mystic, she didn't have the time to care for the mare properly—not if she was going to take Blue to the Olympics.

"But if I do get any money, it's going straight to the Bring Blue to the Olympics Fund," she added in a tight voice, furious all over again with Gabriela.

"Cool," Mitch said. "Well, later. I'm off to fix a couple of fences."

Lyssa saddled up Blue and mounted him, neatly scooping up her boom box from the hood of the tractor. She settled deeply into her saddle as she steered her horse toward the dressage arena. Making her way across the ranch, she could see that the ground was covered with a fresh layer of snow. The arena was covered, too, of course, but it didn't matter. The letters Lyssa had placed all around the perimeter were perched above the snow and were still visible. At the edge of the arena Lyssa turned to set the boom box on top of a stack of crates. Just as they reached the opening, Blue let out a low whicker. It was then that Lyssa saw a horse and rider at the far end.

Who the heck is that? Lyssa thought, squinting in the glare of the bright sunlight bouncing off the snow. *Did I forget that I'd scheduled a lesson for this morning?* She gathered her reins, urging Blue forward.

As they drew closer, Lyssa's breath caught in her throat. It was Tony—on Mystic. They had just completed a ten-meter circle and were now moving out at an extended trot.

Lyssa halted Blue and watched in amazement as the pair continued working down the straightaway, slowing to a sitting trot when they approached the corner. Tony closed his inside leg at the girth so that Mystic bent deeply into the corner. At the precise moment he cued her into a working canter. The pair turned up the diagonal, and Lyssa could see that Tony was trying to get Mystic to execute a flying lead change. Instead she merely sped up, and Tony had to circle around and try again before Mystic complied.

"Mystic's looking good," Lyssa said nonchalantly moments later when Tony rode up to her. "I don't mean to criticize, but you could balance her better for that change if you weren't sitting so far forward. You've spent too much time jumping and not enough time on the flat. Still, you didn't do too badly—for a cowboy."

Tony tipped his hat and grinned, his teeth gleaming brightly against the snowy backdrop. "Thanks for the compliment, teacher," he said.

"Whatever," Lyssa said. "But more to the point: What are you doing on Mystic, and why are you in my arena?"

Tony ran his gloved hands through Mystic's mane. "Well, Mystic and I needed to practice. As you can see, dressage isn't my best discipline."

Lyssa tilted her head. "It's not mine, either," she began, then stopped. "Cut out the evasions. I've got to tell you, I've pretty much had it with you!"

Tony raised his hands, still holding the reins, in a gesture of surrender. "Okay, confession time," he said seriously. "I stole this horse."

Lyssa scowled and shot him a warning look.

"Well, I did," Tony insisted. "Your friend Gabriela sold her to me so cheaply, I might just as well have stolen her."

"She sold her to you?" Lyssa echoed blankly.

"Yep," Tony replied. "For just enough to satisfy the Jockey Club. Transfer of ownership and all that."

Lyssa glanced at the beautiful mare, sadness filling her. "I hate to tell you, Tony. No matter what you paid for her, you didn't get a deal. Gabriela sold her to you cheaply because she's got a lameness issue," she said. "I don't know what causes it, but it could be anything."

Tony nodded. "Gabriela told me all about it, how it comes on sometimes and other times she's sound as anything. I've been studying her feet, and I don't really like the angle of her pasterns. That could be part of what's going on. Anyway, I think I've got some ideas about how I can mitigate the problem."

Lyssa shook her head. "But that doesn't change the fact that if you want to event, Mystic might not be the horse for you. She might not hold up."

Tony shrugged. "Then again, she might," he said. "I took an extension class in corrective shoeing last summer. I think I can do some things with her shoeing to help redistribute the stress on her feet. She's too special. I'm not about to let her slip through my fingers."

Lyssa sighed. "I'm glad," she said quietly. "So that explains why you have Mystic, but it doesn't explain why you're not in Arizona."

"Because I'm staying right here," Tony replied.

"In Montana?" Lyssa was confused.

"Right *here*," Tony repeated. "Part time, anyway. My cousin gave me a part-time job at Huffman Trailers and a place to stay till I can find a more permanent place." He looked straight at Lyssa. "Then on the other

170

days I'll be working here at the Black Thunder. Seems your dad was looking for another hand, and your friend Mitch put in a good word for me."

"Work here?" Lyssa couldn't believe her ears. "Doing what?"

"I'll be rounding up cattle, working with the horses, wiping noses when your dude guests come to stay, and whatever else comes up, I guess," Tony replied.

"You ever worked on a real ranch before?" Lyssa asked, frowning as Blue began dancing around in the cold wind. "Mrs. Peters's place doesn't count, you know."

Tony shrugged. "I was born on Tres Santos near Flagstaff," he said. "We raise Thoroughbreds and purebred Herefords. I guess I've learned a thing or two about livestock over the years." He looked closely at Lyssa. "You don't like the idea of my working here, do you?" he asked softly.

"No, actually, I like it a lot," Lyssa said, dropping her eyes. "As long as you keep Mystic here, that is," she added quickly as she looked up again.

Tony chuckled. "That was part of the deal I worked out with your dad."

"Good," Lyssa exclaimed. "If you can keep Mystic sound, I want to make a real eventer out of her, you know. I think she's got potential."

"How about me? Do you think I've got potential?" he asked.

"As an eventer? Maybe, if you work real hard at your lessons and listen to your instructor," Lyssa tossed back.

Nodding, Tony said, "You don't have to worry about that. I'll definitely work hard. But what I meant was, do you think I've got *potential?*" His eyes locked with hers, till Lyssa turned away.

"It's possible," she said, struggling to keep her voice from shaking.

With that, she turned Blue's head toward the snowy mountains so that Tony wouldn't see her grinning like an idiot.

Woo-hoo! Lyssa thought, squeezing her horse's sides and setting off at a rocking canter through the fresh powder.